CRAZY

CRAZY

LINDA VIGEN PHILLIPS

Eerdmans Books for Young Readers
Grand Rapids, Michigan

This book is first and foremost a work of fiction,
although it is based on real events and real people,
as imagined and interpreted by the author.

Published 2014 by Eerdmans Books for Young Readers,
an imprint of Wm. B. Eerdmans Publishing Co.
2140 Oak Industrial Dr. NE, Grand Rapids, Michigan 49505

www.eerdmans.com/youngreaders

16 17 18 19 8 7 6 5 4 3 2

Library of Congress Cataloging-in-Publication Data

Phillips, Linda Vigen.
Crazy / by Linda Phillips.
pages cm
Summary: While growing up in the 1960s,
Laura uses art to cope with her mother's mental illness.
ISBN 978-0-8028-5437-7
[1. Novels in verse. 2. Mental illness — Fiction.
3. Mothers and daughters — Fiction. 4. Artists — Fiction.] I. Title.
PZ7.5.P52Cr 2014
[Fic] — dc23
2013048058

To my mother, whose fault it
never was, and to my sister,
my soul mate in survival.
— *L. V. P.*

APRIL 1963

BETH'S OPINION

Beth Watson says I'm crazy.

You know how best friends
love to razz you like that,
calling you crazy
when you do something wild.

"Man, Laura, you're crazy,"
she said when I told her
I almost jumped off the 11th Street Bridge
last week, the day of basic colors in home ec
where we were supposed to discover
the color that would bring out our skin tones.
And you can just imagine what it would do
for the zits scattered around our faces
like a bad case of chicken pox.
Mrs. Honeycut made us stand
in the front of the room
in front of all those prissy girls from Tremont —
you know,
from up on the hill where all the fancy big houses are —
the girls who have shoes
to match every outfit.
Honeycut twirled this color chart
right next to my face —
really, right next to my mouth,
like an arrow pointing directly
to my huge front teeth,
which Jerry Pruner already calls
buck teeth.
So everyone in the whole room
focused on my teeth

to determine what my basic color was,
and before you know it
that horrible
heart-thumping feeling started creeping
up from beneath my bra, and I thought,
"God help me, here it comes again,"
and the high collar
on my blouse
did nothing to stop the heat
and color from crawling up my neck —
not evenly, like a sunburn,
but in splotches
like cauliflower gone real bad.
The room got so hot
you could probably cook that cauliflower,
and then those circles started to grow
under my armpits,
but thank goodness, this time
I had the big brown cardigan on —
it matches almost everything I have,
including the penny loafers,
so I didn't have to concentrate
on keeping my arms plastered against my body
so nobody could see the half-moons of sweat.

Then my eyes and ears caught the snickers
starting to circulate around the room —
Penny, Rhonda, Babs,
the cheerleader babes —
and the whispers, I knew,
I just knew for sure,
were not only about my ugly teeth,
my beet-red face,
my splotchy neck,

but the whole way
I completely freak out
every time I get embarrassed,
which lately seems to be
at the rate of every two seconds,
even when I don't have to give a speech.
All I had to do was stand there,
for Pete's sake.
I can just hear Jerry Pruner after class:
"Hey Laura, is that disease all over your neck contagious?"

So the class decided on brown
for my basic color,
as in
mud
rats
rotten bananas
swamp water
and dirty anything.

I ran out the side door after school —
thank heavens home ec was last period —
thinking my cheeks were so hot
they must be leaving a trail of smoke.
I stopped by the canal,
swarming with hungry pelicans
and screeching gulls,
and I wondered,
just wondered and wondered
for I don't know how long,
what it would feel like
not to sit and dangle my feet through the slats
and daydream and watch
like I usually do

but instead to climb up on the railing
and let myself just slip off and down
and down
and down.

I decided against it because,
of course,
I'm not the crazy one
in our family.

MY OPINION

Megan's favorite creature on earth
is her cat,
and whenever anything big happens
with the cat,
Beth, Diane, and I
are the first to hear.

Today at lunch
we barely sat down
when Megan came up,
breathless,
bursting to tell us
what happened over the weekend.

Megan told us between sandwich gulps
how her cat had been missing
since last Friday morning.
It never stays away longer than a few hours,
so they knew something was up.
They posted signs,

scoured the neighborhood,
even knocked on some doors.

Turns out it was trapped
in her next-door neighbor's cellar.
Her dad said it likely squeezed through
a small hole in an air vent next to the furnace
that roars like an outboard motor
when it cycles on and off.
I stopped eating when Megan
did a pretty convincing rendition
of the cat's plaintive cry,
the one that caught her attention
when she took the garbage out last night.
I can picture that cat
cowering in the musty darkness,
terrorized by the unpredictable noise,
unable to make a move,
frozen in fear
wide-eyed
trembling
trapped.

Beth can call me crazy if she wants,
but I'm not
crazy.

I'm more like the cat —
hiding out
at my house,
never knowing what might happen next,
stuck in this body,
in this family,
a little fearful —

no, a lot fearful —
of things
I can't explain.

I can't explain
why rooms get too hot
eyes start to stare
words evaporate
bridges call my name.

But I also can't explain
why I felt so good
dancing cheek to cheek
with Dennis Martin
like I did
at the after-game dance last week.

It stirred up my insides
something fierce
in such a new way,
I almost forgot
I live in the Twilight Zone
somewhere on the other side
of sanity.

BUDDING ARTIST

I work hard at being an artist
mostly because Mrs. Grant,
my favorite teacher,
says if I keep it up
I could be as great

as old Vincent van Gogh.
He's her favorite artist —
though, of course,
I wouldn't want to be quite as great as he was,
because who knows why he cut off his ear.
But if I were *almost* as great as he was,
I probably wouldn't go to such extremes.
Look, if I can keep myself
from jumping in the swirling green canal
on basic color days,
I can certainly refrain from chopping
off body parts.

We practice copying the greats
in art class. Mrs. Grant says
I capture Vincent's swirls
and stars and sunflowers
and golden yellows and brilliant blues
as well as any of the seniors.
"You've got the gift, Laura.
You do your sophomore class proud."

It's not just that I want to be great,
but it's more like
I can't seem to get the pencil to work
in the direction of words or numbers
as well as I can with lines and shapes.
It makes me feel better, too,
because when I'm drawing or painting
the stomachache goes away,
and I never have to go to the nurse
during art class.

I might have a shot

at being at least a little bit great.
I get the art award every year
at school,
and I mean,
no kidding,
my friends, Beth and Megan and Diane,
all come to me
all the time
for artistic advice.
I draw sketches for their projects
for free.
Like last Saturday
I escaped the madhouse
early in the morning
before Mama's first cigarette
and before Daddy could growl at me
for not practicing the flute
or make me go grocery shopping with them
and then sit in the car outside the VFW
with Mama
while he stopped for a shot of whiskey
and I hoped to goodness no one I knew
would come walking by.

Beth and I met at the usual spot
on the bridge.
"Hey, you're late."
She looked up at me over her thick lenses,
and I could tell she was in a hurry
to get to the library today.
"Hold your horses, I've got something for you."

I pulled out my ink sketch of Shakespeare
and for a split second I felt like taking it back

because I kinda liked the way I got his high forehead,
his deep-set eyes, that stylish hairdo,
and especially that one earring.
Mrs. Grant would call it "A+" material
if I do say so myself.

Beth has no interest in drawing or painting herself,
but she claims she's learning how to be an art collector —
starting with my stuff
so she'll be good at it
by the time she's a rich and famous scientist.

"For me?" she asked.
"Fantabulous, my dear. And now . . .
tah-dah!"

She waved the chemistry notes
around in the air
until I snatched them.
I may be less than
a fantabulous scholar,
but I'm mighty glad to have a friend like Beth
to bail me out of the class I hate the most.

BETH

I love Saturdays with Beth,
our work spread out on the back table
in the musty city library,
whispering just under the radar
of the silver-haired librarian at the front desk.
Beth's short, plump fingers

make easy sense
out of math and chemistry equations,
while detailed images emerge
from my swirling, skinny hand.
We've been an unlikely pair
since Mrs. Barry seated us next to
each other on that first day of school.
One tall, one short,
one scientific,
one artistic.
She's made me laugh on days
when laughter seemed impossible.
She's made me laugh at myself.
I need her dry wit,
her rock-solid steadiness,
the easy-going attitude that seems to come
with being a middle child.
I look at her round, clear-skinned face,
realizing not for the first time
how pretty her blue eyes are.
I wonder
sometimes
what I bring
to our friendship.

But I don't waste time today
questioning a good thing,
library time with Beth.

It's the best part of the week
before I have to trudge up the hill
back home.

CERAMICS

Paula and Mama are taking a ceramics class
every week in the basement
of the city library.
They aren't creating ceramics,
just painting unglazed pieces from a mold.
Daddy says it was Dr. Goodman's idea,
to help calm Mama's nerves.

I peeked in once,
and it was spooky.
It was like a city of little ghostly white statues
scattered all over the place
waiting to wake up,
you know,
like the frozen creatures in Narnia
after the White Witch cast her spell,
people and animals
waiting to be released
back into life
and the world of color.

You can see ceramics
from the class
all around Paula's house
and ours.

Paula has a greenish fish on her bathroom wall;
ceramic bubbles of various sizes
float up and away from its mouth,
and colorful vases everywhere
for the tons of green plants
she keeps around the house.

She says they help her breathe
better than she could
in all the cigarette smoke at home.

Our house is cluttered with religious stuff,
the Virgin Mary in a blue robe,
the same powder blue Mary always wears
for the Christmas pageant.
She's holding baby Jesus in that white
swaddling blanket they wrapped him in.
Mama's favorite hangs on the wall
in the dining room.
It's called a frieze.
Jesus sits in the middle of a long table
and the disciples lean toward him
from the right
and from the left,
trying to hear every word.
The scene is famous, from a da Vinci fresco
called *The Last Supper*
found in a monastery
in Italy.
I don't know what colors da Vinci used,
but Mama painted her version
all one boring color
of gold.

I look at her oil paintings,
one in the living room and one in their bedroom,
that she did when she was about my age,
and I wonder how it is
that she has drifted from
creating brilliant oil paintings
to slapping paint on molded figurines.

The painting I like best
(you can see it if you look
just over the top of the TV rabbit ears)
is a bowl full of nasturtiums
in rich, autumn colors.
Mrs. Grant might even say
it has a Rembrandt feeling.
Mama is no Rembrandt,
but she got the golds and browns and oranges
of the nasturtiums just right
with a dark, shadowy background.
Mrs. Grant would love the composition,
how the flowers trail off to the right of center.

"Why don't you take up painting again?"
I ask her one day,
admiring this pleasing arrangement
she created when she was fourteen.

"Oh, I could never get back to that,"
she says, slamming a window
against the rising storm.

THE PELICANS AND LIGHT

My room isn't very big,
but it has northern light
and just enough space for an easel
and all my paint stuff,
especially since I took out the silly frilly
bean-shaped dressing table.
It was something Paula and Mama

thought I should have.
It never really fit me.

Most days when I get home,
unless Dick Clark has someone
out of this world
on *American Bandstand*,
I head straight for my room
and the easel,
my construction zone.
Right now I'm doing a study of the pelican,
our school mascot,
not just because it's an assignment in art class,
but because I love the way it's made peace
with its bizarre body.
Imagine being stuck with that outrageous beak,
about one-fourth as long as its body,
and worse yet, it's on the end of a neck
that can never be raised, has to stay tucked forever
due to a front-end vertebrae arrangement.
Now you take a wingspan twice as long
as the bird's length, put it together
with a short, pudgy body and sagging orange pouch,
and you have what Jerry Pruner would call
one ugly bird.

Today I'm kind of glad I refrained from
taking that dive into the canal last week.
I wouldn't be here to stand back
and enjoy looking at my canvas,
a pleasing arrangement of two pelicans
awash in brightness.
One swims alongside its prey,
poised for a precision dive

into the grimy green water.
The other larger bird soars above,
with the blinding afternoon sun
glancing off silky feathers
like a regular Hopper effect,
you know, how Edward Hopper
uses light just like Vincent uses color
to make his point,
like the overexposed light that just shouts
off his *Lighthouse at Two Lights.*

Mrs. Grant told me how I could send away
to the Met for a poster last year,
and now some of that light
spreads down on me
from its overlook above my bed.
I had hoped it would eat away at the darkness
on the worst sleepless nights,
more and more lately,
when panic
sets in.

What if I don't sleep?
Don't sleep at all?
Don't sleep?
What if?
Sleep?

I had hoped bringing more light
into my room
would scare away
the night ghosts.

I had hoped.

MAMA FORGETS

Even when I'm not painting,
I hang out in my room with the door shut,
Beach Boys spinning on the turntable
loud enough to drown out the dull noise
of things not quite right
on the other side of the wall.
Mama's always been weird,
but lately she's off-the-chart forgetful.

The other day
she lit two cigarettes at once,
and God knows what might have happened
if I hadn't found the one smoldering in the ashtray,
just about ready to drop on the davenport.
The day before that
she couldn't find the iron,
and she worked herself up over it
and made me help her look for it,
and then she collapsed into a pile of tears
when we found it
in the fridge.

Paula says to just laugh it off.
Sure, that's easy enough for her to say.
She doesn't have to live here anymore.
I don't know why she gripes all the time
about how much work it is
taking care of Kim and Jeff.
Good grief, has she forgotten
already
how hard it is
to live here in the loony bin? I mean,

here she's living a fairy-tale life
in her own little house
across town, with a husband and two kids,
I mean, a real life of her own.

What are the chances I'll ever meet
a hunk like her husband Frank
anywhere in this podunk mill town?

The best I can hope for is a logger
who promises to shave off his beard
and clean the sawdust out of his ears
once a week.

Sure, Dennis Martin danced cheek to cheek
with me last week,
but after I lost count of how many others got
the same treatment,
I felt pretty sure dancing with me was a dare
from one of the other jocks.
I mean, why else would someone with
Gregory Peck looks ever give me the time of day?
It's probably my art. Dennis knows
I'm always good for a quick poster
for the pep rallies.
Yeah, that's it.
He was just making sure his art options
stay secure.

Okay, so I try laughing off the cigarette thing
and the iron incident,
but the thing that gets to me the most
is the nothingness of Mama's life,
the absence of anything normal

like playing bridge,
or having lady friends over,
or going to a Tupperware party —
all those things normal mothers do.

Instead
she sits and stares,
rocks and rocks the devil
out of the green rocker,
smokes and stares
stares and paces
paces and mutters
and stares and stares
out those blank eyes through that thick cloud of smoke,
eyes that shut you out of her secret world,
and sometimes
when you do break through,
you know,
you just know,
that she left part of herself on the other side of sanity
and she's trying to remember
where she was when she got lost.

But there is one cool thing
about having a weirdo mother.
She works so hard at remembering
where she left herself,
she doesn't have time
to work on me.

ART CONTEST

Mrs. Grant is all jazzed up in class today,
eyeballing me the whole time.
She's telling us about the annual
Crawford County Chamber of Commerce art contest.
The winner of the teen division
gets a scholarship
to the Art Institute of Portland.
Around these parts
that's like
striking gold.

This year the art show
is hooked up with the annual
Shakespearean festival somehow
with the theme
"To Thine Own Self Be True —
Reflections from My Personal Portfolio."
Mrs. Grant says you can submit what you have
or create a whole new portfolio.
She goes into registration details,
and my mind starts rummaging through my portfolio
like I rummage through my drawers
to find a matching sock.

I think about the charcoal sketch
I did while watching Kim and Jeff
the other day.
Whatever is on my mind
just comes rolling out
as easy as breathing,
and in this case
I sketched my earliest memory

that I had to write about the day before
in English class.

Too bad writing isn't as easy
as sketching.
What I tried to write about was my first trip
to the ocean way back when I was about three years old.
Paula, Mama, and I rolled up our pedal pushers
and Daddy rolled up his khaki pants
and we all walked along the windy beach
scattered with driftwood.

The water was freezing
but Paula and I both dipped our toes in and out
of the water, squealing and laughing like crazy.
We didn't mind getting our feet wet,
but we weren't about to go swimming.
Suddenly a huge wave crashed in
faster than anyone could run.
They all got soaked trying to outrun it
while I hopped up on a gnarly old log
and kept dry.
Grandma was watching from the shore,
and when we all got back to the campfire
she said it was smart
the way I handled that wave.

Well, maybe it's not so big a deal.
I can impress a seven-year-old niece
and four-year-old nephew
with my sketch of the log
stretched out along the shore
with its tangled roots reaching for the sky
and the wave curling around the bottom

and me, a three-year-old,
perched on top like the winner
of king of the mountain.

Maybe it really only matters
that everything from my fingers
to my toes
feels terrific
whenever
my thoughts roll out
in the shape
of a
picture.

DEADLINE

Mrs. Grant's voice calls me back
to the moment.

"Registration is due in June
with the deadline for art submission in January.
Wouldn't it be fun," she says,
looking straight at me,
"to work on it over the summer?"

After class I tell Mrs. Grant
I'm not at all sure
what being true to thine own self really means.

"Study your work, Laura," she says.
"Try to figure out what part of you
shines through on the canvas.

I'll be surprised if you don't bump into
a new awareness of who Laura is."

She puts her hands on her hips
with that look she gets
when she's about to send you to the office,
and then the edge of her mouth
starts quivering into a grin.

"Laura Wahlberg, if you can't make us proud,
I don't know who can."

I sail out of her classroom
and head for Beth's locker,
eager to get *her* take
on who Laura Wahlberg
really is.

FREQUENT CALLERS

I fly out of my room to catch the phone.
It will be Beth again.
She'll want to know what I thought of the algebra test,
and I'll tell her I probably flunked,
even though I probably squeaked by,
and she probably knows it,
but we play the game,
our usual best-friend game,
until she gets to the real point,
our unfinished conversation about the Beatles.
Her older brother listens to the BBC at night,
and he says their song "Please Please Me"

is all over the radio.

"Paul's the grooviest, don't you think?" Beth says.
She's dead serious.

"Is he the one that looks sort of like Dennis Martin
if Dennis let his hair grow out
and started wearing a suit and tie?" I ask,
knowing for sure Beth will jump
on my ignorance
or my taste in guys.
She says Dennis is a loser,
but I think that's only because he has all those prissy girls
hanging all over him all the time.
I mean, it's not his fault.
He's just too nice to tell them to get lost,
that's all.

"Besides the fact that you think every
dark-haired guitar player
is a Dennis Martin look-alike,
yeah, there might be a slight resemblance,
but it's Paul's brainpower I love. He and John
do all the writing
and together their music is
way beyond compare."

All those brothers and sisters come in handy.
Beth always seems to know more
about things going on than I do.

It's amazing when you think about it.
Mrs. Watson has time to be PTA president,
and Mr. Watson can sell cars

and find time to run the school board
and be the father to all those kids
who get all those straight As.

As soon as I hang up the phone
we get another call.
It's Aunt Hazel
checking on Mama
again.
She's getting on my nerves now,
calling twice a day
since spring break
to see how Mama is.
I don't know how nosy Aunt Hazel
found out about our disastrous trip to the coast
because I know darn well
it wasn't old tight-lipped Daddy.
He doesn't give Aunt Hazel the time of day,
let alone tell her
how much fun it was trying to drag
Mama out of the car
to go anywhere,
how she mostly sat and stared —
when she wasn't crying —
and how she didn't eat more than
a piece of lettuce all week.

I wonder
just what kind of read
Aunt Hazel is getting
on our family
with all these stupid
phone calls.

OVERHEARD CONVERSATION

Diane comes running down the hall
in one of the new outfits her mom
made for her. Envy grabs hold of me
before Diane's hand clutches my arm.

"Guess who was talking about you
in biology just now!"

I go cold and brace myself for the worst.
"Let me guess. One of my cheerleader friends?"

"No, silly. Dennis!
His dad just got a new company car,
and Dennis was telling Howie
how he hadn't put a single scratch on the Riviera,
so his dad just handed over the keys and it's
in mint condition and his permit now
allows passengers and, you know how Dennis
goes on and on when he's revved,
well anyway he was telling Howie who he'd
like to take for a ride,
and well, Laur, you are at the top of his list!"

"You mean behind Rhonda and Babs and . . ."

"No, honest, yours was the only name I heard,
and believe me, I was leaning in there
pretending to get my notebook out,
straining for every word,
and I swear,
it was your name.
Hey, I've gotta run.

Just thought you would want to know
before you get that call."

She squeezed my arm,
gave me her gorgeous smile,
and took off down the hall.

"Hey Diane,
I love your outfit!"

INFREQUENT CALLERS

"Hey Laura,
what's happening?"

Gulp.
Silence.
Say something!
Don't let him know you're breathing
— too loud, I mean.
DO NOT COUGH.

"Den . . ." *(NO, DO NOT STAMMER!)*
"Dennis?"

"Hey babe, whatcha up to?"

Pause.
"Uh, not much. You?"

"This is your lucky day, man.
My calendar flipped over today,

reminding me there is some advantage
to being a year older than babes like you,
because my six-month provisional is passé,
and that means I am now taking on passengers,
and the coolest thing of all is
I got a new ride
due to the fact I did not put one dent
in my old man's wheels throughout the whole
permit trip, ya' know?
Yeah, the company updated his wheels —
a cherry red T-Bird — so I got his black Riviera,
you've seen it around,
the hardtop coupe with baby moon hubs?

"How 'bout goin' for a little spin,
whaddya say, just you and me?
I'll swing by 'round seven . . ."

Yes, that's about how it might go

if Dennis calls.

DISSONANCE

The silent, empty halls
nudge me back to reality,
and I pack up for the day,
wishing once again
I could somehow drop band.
It would make my backpack lighter,
maybe make my life lighter.

Less practicing,
more painting.

I come to the same conclusion I always do
when I have this conversation
with myself.

It's Daddy's thing, not mine.

Of course he thinks
I could beat out the competition for first chair
if I'd just practice more.
"If I'd just practice more"
will be the title of my next painting,
and I can already see it shaping up
like Picasso's *Three Musicians,*
all chopped up in nice little cubes
just like my flute sounds
sometimes.

By the time I get home,
my head already throbbing,
I find Mama busy —
not busy sitting in her chair
smoking and reading,
not busy fixing dinner
like some sluggish zombie,
not busy getting ready to start
or finish a good cry —

but busy painting.

"What do you think?"
she says, her animated voice

so out of character
for these recent months.
I am speechless.
I try to remember the last time
I saw her this keyed up,
or when I last saw her
paint.

The picture she has apparently
just finished,
or maybe just barely started,
reflects the frenzy
all around the room.
I can't make sense out of it
or my own thoughts.

"It's, um, nice," I say, "but why
today? I mean, where did all this
come from, so suddenly,
today?"

"Well, why not today? Wasn't it your idea
that I take up painting again?
You know I'm an artist.
I thought you would be glad
to see me using my talent again.
Be a good girl now,
and hand me that rag. I just
have time to finish this up
before I start dinner."

I hand her the rag
and stare in disbelief
at this strange person —

my mother,
who has gone from docile to demanding
overnight.

I retreat to my room to figure out
what's wrong with this picture,
why I'm not feeling
glad my mother loves art.

STORM BREWING

I can't stand it any longer,
living in the same house with her.
After weeks and weeks
of blah nothingness
I now have a mother
with enough energy
to power the city of Crawford Hills.
Suddenly she has transformed
from sitting listlessly in her chair
to constantly moving
fidgeting
pacing
talking to herself and
painting
painting
painting
wild,
scary-looking pictures.

She's inside right now,
staring out the window muttering something

about needing to watch for the cars,
and I'm thinking, what cars
is she watching for on this lonely dirt road
that maybe sees a car every few hours?
It's as if she's waiting for someone to pick her up
and take her somewhere,
which we all know is not the case
because she has no friends
and besides, it's almost dark.
To top it off,
Daddy just sits there in his chair,
behind the newspaper,
never saying a word,
acting as if everything is fine,
when you know
something is really haywire with his wife.
It's driving me crazy!

So I come out here on the porch,
too rattled to even think about sketching.
I come out
to breathe,
to let the cool April air wash over me,
to watch the thunderheads roll in over
my favorite mountains,
the ones that always remind me of an old Indian chief
lying on his back
with his hands across his chest
like he's sleeping peacefully,
and I can smell the wild sage growing
in the field across the road,
and the crisp air feels good
on my hot cheeks,
and the sky,

lit up like Monet's *Haystacks*,
calms the uneasiness that has my gut twisted up
like someone has punched me
with an iron fist.

Maybe it's finally getting to Daddy, too.
I can hear his hammer now
out in the shed
bang, bang, banging
so hard and fast and thunderous.
I wonder if he's working on the desk
he promised me,
or if he's using the hammer to speak
the only way he knows how

and I wonder
if he senses the storm coming on
like I do.

RELIGION

One really screwy thing
about our family is religion.
Maybe it's because it's always
the first thing Mama turns to
and the last thing on Daddy's mind.
Don't get me wrong,
I have nothing against religion.

Look, I know the daughter of the pastor at
Trinity Lutheran.
She's just as zany

as the rest of us.
I see her cruising Main after the movies,
and she's always hollering out the window,
waving at Dennis Martin.
Frankly, I think she's madly in love with him,
although I personally don't think he's her type.
Well, maybe I really mean
she's not his type.

He's not the jerk
everyone, especially Beth,
says he is.
It always looks like he's drooling all over
those slutty cheerleaders
when really,
he's just a friendly guy.
That's how he gets the reputation,
when girls start spreading rumors
about how much of a make-out he is.
I don't believe it all, anyway.
I think the other jocks are just jealous of him,
and that's why they call him "88 Fingers."
I don't care what they say.
He can't be that nice to me in history class
and be all that bad.
Can he?

But back to religion.
Things are really nuts in that department
at our house.
Get this. Daddy says
he's a member of Crawford Lutheran,
which is a whole lot different from Trinity.
He would have a hard time

drinking all his beer
over at Trinity.

Most of the time Daddy drops me off
and picks me up after the ten o'clock service,
which is fine with me,
because then I can sit in the gallery with my friends
and draw
and half-listen to the sermon
and whisper
without being shushed by an adult.

On Saturday night,
Daddy drives over to 7th Street
and finds a good parking spot
outside Sacred Heart Catholic
and waits while Mama goes to confession
and then to the five o'clock mass.
When Paula was still home,
she went with Mama,
while I sat out in the car with Daddy
and drew pictures and waited.

For some dumb reason
they decided early on
that Paula should be Catholic
and I should be Lutheran.
They must have tossed a coin or something
or chosen sides,
like in a spelling bee —
you take this one,
I'll take that one.

A while back I asked Mama

why we don't all go to the same church.
"So Daddy can see you're brought up proper
in the church," she said,
"in case something happens to me.
Paula's old enough to take care of herself now,
with her own family and all.
And when she was younger,
before you were born, well —
I felt a lot stronger
than I do now."

I'll be the first to tell you
that a lot of things about religion
just don't make sense,
but this makes the least sense of all —

trying to figure out what
might happen to Mama.

SLUMBER PARTY

The four of us sprawl on sleeping bags
lined up on the plush new carpet
of Megan's living room,
the one room in the old Victorian house
that her contractor father is
renovating. While it's definitely
the largest house of all of ours,
even Megan jokes about
when it might ever be finished,
since all his other work comes first.

Megan tries to avoid choking
to death on the popcorn
while Beth, Diane, and I
take turns filling in the stories
about the days before Megan moved to our district,
when we gave our teachers fits
with the alphabetical seating arrangement
that permanently glued us together.

It was always
Diane Vance, Laura Wahlberg, Beth Watson . . .
that's how I came to sit between
my two best friends
in almost every class we had together.

"Hey Laur, we never heard how
the phone call went," Diane says,
taking ladylike nibbles of popcorn.

Now it's my turn to choke.
"That's because it didn't."

Gasps.

Beth says it's confirmed:
Dennis is the jerk she always
thought he was.

She says I'm just too good for him. He doesn't
know what to do with a brain if it's not attached
to a sexy body. No offense, Laur.

Megan says he's just waiting for the right moment.
Coughs, giggles, and snickers.

Diane says he's given in to
the snooty Tremont crowd up on the hill. They're all
rooting for Rhonda, you know.

I crawl into the sleeping bag,
relieved that my friends have solved
my love life
without a single word
from me.

CONFIRMATION PLANS

I know it's supposed to be an honor
giving half of the confirmation speech
while Diane does the other half.
She's supposed to talk about the sacraments,
like what it means to be baptized
and take communion,
and why we say the Apostles' Creed every week,
and what all the prayers mean,
and I'm supposed to talk about what a ruckus
old Martin Luther made when he tacked those
ninety-five theses on the church door,
telling the pope that he had it all wrong.
And then we come to why
Diane and I are standing up there
in the first place,
which is to make a public announcement
that we understand all the stuff
we've learned in Sunday school all these years
and we are ready to speak for ourselves
about what we believe,

you know, to confirm that what our parents
said we would do at baptism
really came through.

But to tell you the truth,
I'd sooner die a heathen
than stand in front of that whole congregation
and profess my faith
while I'm wondering what
my wacky mother is going to do next.
How am I supposed to concentrate
on my speech
when I have to worry
about whether she will decide to
slump over in the pew
or stand up and babble?
I hate making speeches anyway.

She has to get written permission
from the Catholic bishop
to step inside Crawford Lutheran
for my confirmation
in the first place.
Maybe I'll luck out,
and he'll just say no.

But if the answer is yes,
she'll be there.

God knows Mama takes her religion
much more seriously
than Daddy does.

RITE OF PASSAGE

"So Laura, babe, you look
like glum with a capital *G*
today. What's up?"
Dennis says, twirling his pencil
and jiggling his foot to
separate beats while we wait
for Werner
to shuffle in,
clear his throat,
and commence with American history.

I blush
as usual
and think about
asking him not to call me "babe"
as usual
but decide against it
as usual
and then half-answer the question
as usual.

"I have to do this stupid confirmation stuff
at church, and well,
you know,
I really hate,
you know,
getting up in front of a large group,
you know?"

"Serious?
Come on, now! Someone as smart as you
shouldn't have a problem with that."

I look him square in the eye
and come dangerously close
to telling him I am smart enough
to know what a huge jerk he is,
but then I remember that I'm
not really supposed to know that
he was talking about me
or even thinking about me
(if he really was
even thinking about me),
and I can feel the splotches blooming
on my neck, and
suddenly I feel very warm,
and I'm not sure if it is because
Dennis just said a very nice thing to me —
or at least I think it was nice —
while I was thinking un-nice things
about him,
or something else is going on,
because I am warm all over.
When Werner sidles through the door,
I almost knock him down
asking for a hall pass
to the restroom
quick,
and when I get there
I find
I've finally gotten my period.
I spend a very long time
in the bathroom trying to take care of things
and pulling my hair away from behind my ears
to hide my beet-red face.
I soak a paper towel with cold water
and try to cool off.

Man, how I hate my multicolored
neck. I pull my collar up as far as it will go,
slip back into the classroom,
and slide down in my seat,
horrified that this whole episode
is probably written all over me
like the scarlet letter.

I can feel Dennis staring at me
as I race out of class without
looking at him.

"You look flustercated, kiddo,"
Beth says when I meet up
with her and Diane at the lockers.
When I tell them what happened,
Diane says, "About time,"
since she and Beth both beat me to it long ago.

"Go home and talk girl talk
with your mom," Diane says, laughing.
"She'll make it all better."
She tosses her mane of thick, dark brown curls
and flashes her flawless smile.
Easy enough for her to say.
Her mom, our Girl Scout leader
since we all started out as Brownies,
acts normal
sounds normal
looks normal
is normal.

"Yeah, sure," I say, waving them off.
Yeah, sure.

Mama sits in the backyard
under a bright yellow sun,
smoking a cigarette
and swinging her foot in that
nervous way that she does.
She's totally consumed
by a fresh, wet painting
propped up in front of her.

In a voice both flat and absent,
she tells me the supplies
are in the hall closet.
When I come back outside,
thick cumulus clouds have
rolled in, casting a shadow
across our yard.

Something about the frenzied look in her eyes
and the nervous swaying foot
tells me now is no more the time
for girl talk than it ever is.

I head for my room,
take up my flute,
begin blowing out "Some Enchanted Evening"
in long, angry breaths,
while I try to decide
if Dennis Martin
really does look anything
at all like Paul McCartney.

TO THINE OWN SELF BE TRUE

It's Friday, and Sandra,
my favorite cousin,
gets to spend the night
while her mom takes Sandra's sister
to a swim meet
over in Ashland.

We pop corn in the skillet
and watch Lawrence Welk
with Mama and Daddy.
Mama has at least stopped the pacing
and sits down. After a while,
neither of them looks sleepy,
so we decide to go to bed.

In the dark
we share secrets.
I tell Sandra about my period.
She's only a month older,
but she already knows more about it
than I do,
so I switch to art.
I know more about art than she does.
I tell her how it feels
as if my drawings drop out of the sky
like a pelican zooming in on its prey.
"Take the painting I'm working on now,"
I say. "I become the pelican, and well,
the painting just sort of takes off."

I try to explain about the art contest
and being true to yourself,

but I can feel her losing interest.
"Maybe I will win the art contest,
make it big
someday."

Then it's her turn.
She tells me more
about her plans to be a nun
and how she talks to the Virgin Mary
on a regular basis.
She lays out detailed plans,
beginning with the novitiate
on through to final vows.
I listen to the fire behind her words
with my eyes closed,
not falling asleep
but becoming wider awake,
forming a vivid picture in my mind
of Sandra in a flowing black habit,
sparkly eyes
deep-set and mischievous,
her pretty face framed by
that white thing
she calls a wimple.
I want to jump out of bed
and capture my cousin
Sandra the nun
on canvas,
so sure I am that she will fulfill her dreams,
be what she wants to be
someday.

I admire her
even though my own father

calls her "simple" and
seems to make light
of her religious
ways.

"I think they went to bed," she finally whispers.
"Let's sneak outside and look at the stars."
We get as far as the back door
when a stern voice commands
from out of the dark kitchen,
"Get back to bed now and go to sleep."

We spend the next half hour
stifling nervous giggles. "Your father
is scary mean. He was mad,
wasn't he?" she says.

"He's not scary mean
or mad at all. That's just the way he is."

You should see
my mother lately,
I think,
if you want to see
something scary.

Long after Sandra's breathing
evens out into sleep,
I lie awake thinking about
being true to yourself.

I think about Mama and *her* art,
me and *my* art,

Daddy and *his* religion,
Sandra and *her* religion.

Mirror mirror
on the wall,
who's the *truest*
of them all?

LATE NIGHT PROWLER

Two nights after Sandra's visit
I sit bolt upright in bed,
heart pounding wildly.
Something crashed out in the living room.
I hold my breath and wait for other sounds,
when I notice the sliver of light
under my door.

I slip out of bed and
grab my music stand,
ready to hurl it at the burglar,
when I hear the low rumbling sound
of Mama,
clearing her throat
like she does in the morning
after the first cigarette and cup of coffee.
Did I oversleep? Is it time to get up?

The clock on my bureau says 3:30 a.m.
I'm still clutching the music stand
and shaking like crazy
as I creep out of my room and find her

sitting at her usual place at the table,
smoking, with a cup of coffee.

"Mama, what's wrong?"

She jerks in her chair,
as startled to see me
as I am to see her.

"Oh honey, did I wake you?
Just a headache,
that's all.
You don't need
to worry
about me.
I'm fine."

She has that weird,
faraway look in her eyes
that I've seen so often recently,
and her voice
sounds like one of Uncle Ned's
warped records,
sing-songy and high-pitched.
I see a broken picture frame
on the table next to a ripped-up picture,
and my heart lurches
when I realize
it's the nasturtiums.
She's ripped up her own painting,
the nearly perfect one,
the nasturtiums,
and she's destroyed
their perfect arrangement

forever
on the nearly Rembrandt canvas,
and now they lay scattered
across the dirty tablecloth
like crumbling, dried-up flowers.

Suddenly
I feel
like throwing up.

"Why, Mama? Why did you do that?
Why did you ruin
your best work?"

"Oh, there's much more where that
came from, Laura, especially since
you suggested I start painting again.
You just wait and see.
Now go on back to bed
and don't you worry.
Everything is just fine, honey.
Just fine."

MAY 1963

DELIVERY

I'm up way earlier than usual
so Daddy can take the pelicans and me to school
before he catches his ride to the mill.

In the dim light I half dance
around the canvas
while I pull on my clothes,
checking out the painting from every angle,
and I shiver,
not from the early spring chill,
but from something deeper inside,
something about the way the pelicans
carry themselves,
the one soaring,
the other fishing,
the strength and determination,
yes, even the beauty —
and then I stop myself
and quickly finish dressing.
My thoughts switch to Vincent
and I wonder again,
as I often have,
how he came to the point
of self-butchering and ultimately
self-destruction.
Why weren't his twelve yellow sunflowers
or his swirling, starry night
or his billowing cypress trees
reason enough to dance around
with pride, too?
Or worse yet,
was the exhilaration

more than his tortured self
could absorb?

Daddy hollers at me that it's time to go,
and I carefully load the pelicans
into the beat-up Studebaker.
At least it will be early enough
when he drops me off
so that anyone I might know,
especially Dennis,
won't see the reason I walk the mile
to school every day.
I sit outside the main entrance,
engrossed in a gorgeous
cotton-candy-pink sky,
until Beth and Diane show up.

"Oh, we're just in time for
a sneak preview of the winning piece!"
Diane shrieks. Her genuine enthusiasm
brings on a blush to match the sky.
I marvel at her pom-pom spirit.
Even though she's never
expressed the slightest interest in cheerleading,
that's the role she's always taken with us.

They crowd around me,
one on either side,
trying to maneuver me
and the pelicans into the best light.

Beth gasps. "You've done it again, Laur.
It's stupendous.
Are you sure you didn't go ahead

and jump into the canal
that day, after all? To get this kind of
depth and perspective
you must have, well, um,
experienced the canal firsthand."
She nudges my elbow.
"Come on. You can tell us. Did you?"
I glare at her in disbelief. I had told her
about my almost-dive into the canal
in secret. Not that it really matters
that Diane knows, but the fact that Beth
insinuates that I actually did it . . .
I let it go and decide to give her heck later.
Anyway, I know Beth means business
with her compliment
when she goes out on a limb to use a word
besides fantabulous.
Now my heart is picking up speed,
and I start worrying already
about whether Mrs. Grant's appraisal
will match theirs. After all,
they are only my two best friends.

They walk me to the art room,
lurking around outside to listen
while I nervously tiptoe in.
"Well, good morning, Laura," Mrs. Grant says.
"Is this what I think it is?"

I'm not sure what she thinks it is,
so I smile lamely and turn it around
with jerky, shaking hands, and almost drop it.
She clasps her hands in a praying position
and takes a deep, deep breath

while her eyes move all over the canvas.
I wonder for what seems like forever
if it's a sigh of disappointment or delight.
Finally, "How did you do it, Laura?"
I look at her to see if she's being serious,
because I feel like being flip
and saying, "Well, dummy, with oil paint,"
and then she goes on. "I mean,
how did you get those pelicans
to exude so much — so much life?"

"Well, I hang out at the canal a lot."
Now I'm close to breaking out in
nervous giggles,
because a vivid picture of myself flying
over the edge with wings
forms in my mind.

"It's one of your best, if not *the* best ever, Laura,"
she says, looking straight into my eyes. "And tell me,
did you learn anything new about yourself?"

Even though I knew she was going to ask me that question,
I am unprepared. All I can come up with is,
"There is beauty in ugliness."
It must have been the right answer, because
her smile is big.

"We'll talk some more when you fill out
those registration forms for the contest. I'm proud
of you, Laura. Really proud."

ART EXHIBITION

First thing inside the door
I smell turpentine.
I nearly trip over a wet canvas
propped against the door frame.
I follow a trail of smudgy rags
and scattered paint tubes
into the living room,
where I find Mama,
her back to me,
kneeling
muttering
crossing herself
before a dripping canvas.
She's been painting again!

"Hail Mary, full of grace . . . "

A sickening sense of panic begins
crawling up my spine.
"What's going on, Mama?" I ask.

"Holy Mary, Mother of God . . ."

I'm not sure she heard me,
so I move toward her,
bending down to look into her face,
and I say it slower
louder
trying to connect with her eyes.
"Mama, what's . . . going . . . on?"

"Holy Mary, Mother of God . . ."

I reach out to shake her,
maybe even slap her,
do something to snap her out of it,
and get her attention,
when she stops
abruptly,
faces me,
looking past me
somewhere,
signaling me
to be silent.
"Mary's my sister,
see.
She's coming,
coming for a visit . . . and I,
I must finish getting the house
ready for her visit.
Be a good girl now, won't you?
Go clean your room
so you will be ready
when she comes,
see,
ready when she comes,
when Mary comes to our house,
see, when Mary —
Oh, I can't find my orange hue
and I need it —
I have to have it NOW,
have to paint, now, NOW!
Do you see it here
somewhere?
So I can paint Mary
before she comes,
see . . ."

She passes grubby hands absently
through her disheveled hair,
leaving multicolored streaks
and smudges on her face,
and she begins crawling on the floor,
agitated, frantic,
looking for the missing paint
or who knows what.

The clock says Daddy won't be home
for another hour.
I call Paula, but she has to pick Kim up at school.
She says to get Mama quiet
until Daddy comes home,
and then call her back.

Then it hits me.
This is my fault.
I caused this.
I pushed her over the edge,
oh my God,
I did this.
It was my suggestion,
"Take up painting again," I'd said —
oh my God . . .

I clean up the mess as best I can,
finally get Mama to sit down in her rocker.
Still paint-splattered,
she rocks
back and forth
humming,
muttering,
staring past me

without recognition.
I watch her rock
almost in rhythm
with the ticking wall clock,
and I take deep breaths
trying to match the rhythm,
trying to beat down
the panic
surging through
my body.

DESPAIR

Daddy calls Dr. Goodman
as soon as he gets home.
I watch Mama sit listlessly
in the rocker,
and I listen to Daddy clear his throat
more than once
before taking off in a quivering voice
to describe his wife's bizarre behavior
to this doctor
who birthed me
and my niece, nephew, and cousins,
who has taken care of our family all these years,
who has tried everything under the sun
to help Mama.

Sure it's been bad before,
the depression,
bouts of crying,
sleeplessness, restlessness,

lack of appetite —

but not like this,

not the crazy talk,
rambling on about things
that make no sense,
waiting for people who don't exist
to pick her up,
frenzied bursts of activity
followed by periods of nothingness,
not recognizing any of us,
not responding
when we try to get through to her.

Daddy's face is cement-gray
as he hangs up the phone.

"She'll need to go to Salem," he says,
"but it will take a day or two
for a bed to come open."

Salem? Salem where all the
nuts go? Salem the crazy house?
Salem the butt of everyone's
crazy jokes? You mean
Salem,
the
State
Mental
Hospital?

Daddy goes on making arrangements.
Maybe Aunt Hazel can help out

until the hospital can take Mama,
and maybe
I could find something
in the kitchen
for us to eat
and then try
to do my homework,
and

homework?

Good grief,
my own mother
is on her way
to the nut farm,
and I'm supposed to fix dinner
and do my homework
as if nothing is out
of the ordinary?

I go into the kitchen
with my head pounding
and try to make sense out
of food. It's all I can do
to calm down enough to make
cheese sandwiches, watching through
the open door to see what
she is doing,
or not doing.
She hasn't budged
from the rocker
where I left her.
Nothingness.

Maybe that's good
for now.
My hands shake as I bring
the food to the table.
I want to cry instead of eat,
but I know that won't do
right now.
Daddy hates tears.
He always says big girls
don't cry.

He leans into the food
and says it's good.
That's all he says, that the food is good.
She comes to the table,
but doesn't look at the food on her plate.

After dinner I try to do homework
behind my closed bedroom door
but I hear her muttering and pacing —
window
rocker
window
rocker
window
rocker . . .

Somehow, toward midnight
Daddy gets her to bed,
and we all collapse.

NERVOUS BREAKDOWN

If you've ever been there
when a lightbulb gets real bright
just before it blows out,
then you know what it was like
around here when things got extremely crazy,
right before they shipped Mama off
to the nut house.

It's all my fault
for suggesting
she take up painting again.
That's what she was doing
that day I came home
to such a mess.
She was trying to paint on canvas,
not ceramics,
and maybe,
well, maybe she just forgot
how to do it
and it frustrated her real bad.
I could see she was beside herself
with frustration.

I never should have suggested it.

Maybe that's why she put her hand
on the hot stove last night
and didn't even smell
the burning flesh.
Now on top of her craziness
she has a bandaged hand.

And then, in the middle of dinner —
meatloaf that Paula brought —
she says in a perfectly normal voice,
"How long have I been like this?"
I wanted to think a miracle
had just happened,
but Daddy gave me a look that said
"don't get your hopes up"
and kept right on eating.
A few minutes later
she stood up,
knocked her chair over,
and threw her plate on the floor,

so I knew there was no miracle.

Dr. Goodman calls it a
nervous breakdown
and says she will be gone
for maybe a month.

A TREE FULL OF MEMORIES

Daddy says Paula
has enough to do
with Frank and the two kids,
and she can't bring meatloaf every night,
so he sends me down the hill
to stay with Aunt Hazel and Uncle Ned,
just until Mama gets back home.

"Put your things in the back bedroom

and go on outside.
Uncle Ned won't be home for another
half hour," Aunt Hazel says,
looking me up and down
like she always does,
as if she can see right through me
down to my bare bones.

Thankful for an excuse
to escape her piercing eyes,
I shove my few belongings
under the old cast-iron bed
and slip outside to my favorite spot,
the giant old willow
with the low-hanging branch
that forms a bench
as it runs along the ground
before turning skyward.
After a good rain like today,
a puddle forms where this branch
joins two others.

I lean over to check my reflection,
and before I know it I'm sobbing
like a baby.
Big, blubbery tears
splash into the puddle,
my whole body
shuddering,
and I'm gasping for air,
and I'm sure Aunt Hazel will hear,
but I don't really care,
and for a few minutes
I can't stop,

don't want to stop
until I get it all out —
days and weeks
of locked-up sadness.
When the storm finally stops,
I look into the puddle again,
and instead of tears,
a flood of memories
comes rolling out —
things I haven't thought about
in years.
I figure I must have been about five years old
the first time I stayed here.

It had started with a game Mama and I played
one afternoon before Daddy got home.
Mama told me to go get my brush,
my blanket,
the purse Grandma gave me,
some tinker toys,
my favorite book,
because we were going on a trip.
I remember laughing,
running to get each item she named.
When Daddy got home
I ran to him,
pointing to my stuff
scattered across the coffee table,
excited to tell him the news.
Daddy got angry,
and I don't remember what happened then,
but the next thing I knew,
I was staying here
with Aunt Hazel and Uncle Ned.

Mama had taken the trip
without me.
When she got back from her trip,
I went back home,
but all Mama wanted to do
was sit in the big green chair
and stare out the window.
Grandma had to come
and cook dinner.

"Go talk to your mother, now,"
Grandma said one day.
I circled the chair
round and round,
but I couldn't get her attention.
I took some of my favorite things
to her, just like that day
we had played the game,
but Mama didn't want to talk
or play the game,
so I went outside
and played so hard
I fell and scraped my knee.
When I came in all bloody and screaming,
Grandma scooped me up
like a huge bulldozer
and whisked me into the bathroom
to clean me up.
I started kicking and screaming,
trying to push away Grandma
and her giant iron arms —

arms that prevented me
from showing my wound to Mama.

AUNT HAZEL'S HOUSE

Aunt Hazel calls us to dinner
and bustles around the table
all fussy, like it's some kind of holiday celebration.
I figure she's nervous having me here.
She speaks directly to Uncle Ned,
well into his third beer.

"You remember Megan,
Laura's friend down the street?
She's having a little get-together tonight,
and Laura's going to go."

I stare at her in disbelief.
How like Aunt Hazel to remember
something I had only mentioned to her in passing,
something all but lost
in the craziness of this week.
Of course, I can just hear Aunt Hazel
checking with Paula
to see if she thought the party was all
on the up-and-up,
the two of them together
trying to be my mother,
but Aunt Hazel
the detective
must have satisfied her curiosity.

"Boys there, huh? You better do
somethin' with that stringy hair
of yours." Uncle Ned's tongue has
started to loosen. "And watch out they don't
try to slip some liquor

into your Coke."

Aunt Hazel jumps up
from the table,
making a lot of noise
clearing the dishes.

"I'll be ready in a few minutes,"
I tell her.
My heart does a flip-flop
at the thought that
Dennis Martin will probably be there.
I can't help smiling as I
zip up my favorite dress,
the lavender one
with ricrac around the neck,
the high-collar neck just in case
those splotches
start in, especially
when I see Dennis, or, heaven forbid,
someone starts asking all sorts of questions
about why I'm staying with Aunt Hazel.
Good ol' Aunt Hazel.
She means well, even if she is a bit nosy.

She walks me the two blocks down
in the dark
with a flashlight.
"Be ready by ten,"
she says.
I nod and quickly wave her off
before Megan opens the door.
The last thing I need
is for everyone to be asking me

why my aunt is escorting me
to the party.
In case someone does ask, though,
I've got it all figured out
what I'll say.
I'll say my mother
has a rare blood disease,
and she had to go to Portland
for some special medical attention.
Nothing life-threatening,
you know,
and she'll probably be gone
maybe a month.
In the meantime,
I'll be staying with my
Aunt Hazel and Uncle Ned.
No big deal.

DAY DREAMS

Aunt Hazel says I can ride my bike
out to the lake after school
as long as I am home
by dinner.

"Bring me a sketch of those mountains of yours,"
she hollers after me.
Instinctively
I grab the sketch pad
and just as quickly bury it
and Aunt Hazel's words
under the bed.

For the first time,
maybe ever,
I have no desire to sketch
at all.

Songs from *South Pacific*
run through my head.

> *Happy talk, keep talkin' happy talk,*
> *Talk about things you'd like to do.*
> *You got to have a dream,*
> *If you don't have a dream,*
> *How you gonna have a dream come true?*

and without any effort at all
I can feel
the stubble of Dennis Martin's cheek
next to mine.
Beth says that same cheek
connected with at least two others
before I got there.
But, I reminded her,
I'm the one he talked to
for over an hour.

The warm spring sun on my back
makes me feel all tingly,
like snuggling under a huge towel
after a warm bath.

I can hear motorboats
pulling into the marina as I park
my bike by the lagoon.
The sun is sitting high above
the old Indian chief's head,
so I know I have some time.

Across the lagoon a mechanic
surrounded by screwdrivers and wrenches
in the boathouse
leans over an outboard motor,
tinkering
until it sputters
starts
stops
races too loud
then settles into a reasonable whir.

Somehow it makes me think of my mother,
broken and in need of repair.

I let myself wonder
for a little while
what kinds of tools
and expertise
it takes to fix
a nervous breakdown,

but I can't stay there long,
at least not today.
That line of thinking
takes me down into a dark hole.

Today I'm a cockeyed optimist.
I hop back on the bike
shrieking at the top of my voice,

> *When the sky is a bright canary yellow*
> *I forget ev'ry cloud I've ever seen,*
> *So they called me a cockeyed optimist*
> *Immature and incurably green.*

FEELINGS

Daddy eats with us sometimes.
He comes and goes,
never lets on
how he feels.

Paula calls every other day,
tells me all about
what Jeff and Kim
are up to.
Not a word about
how she feels
other than the usual —
tired.

Aunt Hazel is too busy
being my substitute mother
to pay any attention
to her own feelings.
Uncle Ned, that's an easy one.
He takes care of his feelings
with a bottle.

Mama. I wonder if she is able
to feel anything
at all.
And me?
I wish feelings
were as simple
as applying paint
to a canvas.

SECRETS

"Hey Laura!" Diane hollers to catch
up with me on the way to history.
"I saw you and Dennis talking
forever
in that dark corner at Megan's party."
She's laughing
but also fishing for something.

"All about art, Diane. He wanted
to know if I could make a bunch
of posters for the pep rally Friday,
that's the long and short of it."

Well, really that's the *short* of it,
while the *long* of it stays buried inside
for fear it will disappear before my eyes.

Dennis had driven the conversation
with what seemed like genuine interest:
Where did you learn to draw like that?
Where do you get your ideas?
What are you going to do with it after high school?
Do you realize how talented you are?

I sat in stunned silence.
Did he really want to know
or was he just making conversation?

I can still picture his eyes
locking onto mine.
"I really want to know what makes
Laura tick."

I really want to know . . .

Diane's voice playfully cuts through my thoughts:
"Sure he just wanted posters,
practically smothering you over in that corner."
She's in a jolly mood
for someone who is probably
bursting with jealousy at
this very moment.
"I'm telling you the truth, Diane.
I'm sorry, but my head is pounding today."

"Okay, okay. I'm sorry, too. I heard about
your mom. Some kind of blood disease, huh?
Is it serious? Will she be all right?"

"Yeah. I mean no. I mean she's not
going to die or anything."

I pick up my pace
like getting to Werner's
next great lecture is
foremost on my mind.

Look,
I really didn't lie to her.

Just answered her questions.

HUNGER

Daddy brings me home

from Aunt Hazel's
for Friday night
because we are going to the hospital
early in the morning
to see Mama.

He sits on the kitchen stool
having one-maybe-two beers,
and I stand in her place
at the sink,
peeling potatoes.

I can't believe it when he breaks his own rule
and starts crying, telling me how much
he loves her. I join him even though
I know it might upset him more.
I want him to keep going
with the feelings because
my hunger for reasons
and understanding
and answers
is far greater
than for
potatoes.

MAYBE IT'S BECAUSE . . .

I think I am beginning to understand
the *nervous* part.
It scares me because
that's how I feel as we drive
to Salem, to the crazy house

to see my mother who had
a nervous breakdown.
What I don't understand
is the *breakdown* part.
What parts broke
and how are they going to fix them?

And what do you say
to a nervous breakdown patient
when you aren't sure how you feel
about her in the first place?

When I look at Daddy across the car seat,
I am afraid he will start crying again,
so I fill up the car with so much
chatter you'd think a flock of anxious starlings
had hitched a ride.

We are greeted in a huge hallway
by a shuffling old lady with a silly grin
saying over and over,
"Maybe it's because the sun is shining,
maybe it's because the sun is shining."

I study dust particles in a shaft of light
and imagine Tinker Bell
spreading enough pixie dust
so I can escape
before my mother arrives.

Suddenly I see another figure entering
the hallway from a side door,
a woman,
not shuffling,

but walking haltingly, burdened
by heavy black shoes.
Smoothing oily hair with one hand,
tugging at a baggy green shift dress with another,
she is almost upon us
before I realize

this is my mother.

"Hello, Harold," she says,
wringing her hands.
He hugs her and clears his throat.

"Iris, you look, you look . . .
are they treating you okay here?"

She turns to me,
hugs me hard,
begins to sob.
"Honey, I miss you so much.
I want to come home."

I don't cry
or return the hug
or say a word.
Daddy lets her cry it out.
"The doctor says
he needs more time, Iris."
He speaks in a tone
more calm and gentle
than I've ever heard.
We spend the rest of the time
on small talk.

Daddy and I drive home in silence.
I close my eyes against the glaring sun
and try to remember what my mother
used to look like.

REVELATION

Good news!
Aunt Hazel hangs up the phone
to announce that Paula just got that big promotion
she's been trying for.
It means extra money,
and that's got to be a good thing for them.

At least I thought it was good news
until Aunt Hazel lights a cigarette
and says, "Humph, just more
for your mother to worry about.
She spends all her time
worrying about you and Paula.
She'll worry herself to death
that the promotion will be too much
for your strong, sturdy sister.
She worries about everything
and see, it's made her sick."
I stare out the window
through Aunt Hazel's freshly
laundered curtains
and consider this new piece
of information.
Not the news about the promotion,
but about my mother.

It's not like I didn't know before now
that my mother worries.
It's just that I never connected it
with good things
like new jobs,
and I never realized how it consumes her.
How we consume her.

She spends all her time
worrying about you and Paula.
I wonder what it is about me
that worries Mama
right now?

Suddenly I feel dirty,
like a virus
capable of making
my mother sick
no matter what I do.

DECISIONS

I lie in my own bed,
not on Aunt Hazel's lumpy old spring mattress,
and I realize how much I have missed
familiar things,
like the way my bed hugs my body,
the way the sun sparkles on the birch tree leaves,
how the mountains are framed
by my pink curtains,
and the familiar sound of the meadowlark
on the telephone wire

outside my window.

After her month-long absence,
Mama came home yesterday,
unfamiliar from head to toe.
New hairdo
new smile
new walk
new gaze
new way of talking
new routine.
She has to take naps
and a pile of new pills.

I made two decisions
based on her homecoming.

Since she bears no resemblance
to Mama, I will call her Mother

and

I'm not going to confirmation
if she has to come along.
Someone else will just have to stand up
in front of the whole congregation
and profess the faith.

I snuggle down under the covers
and wish I could stay here
forever.

JUNE 1963

LAST DAY

It's the last day of school,
the last day of my sophomore year,
the last day to feign interest in
Werner's boring monologue
while Dennis Martin's aftershave
teases my nose,
the last day to whisper secrets at the locker
with Beth and Diane,
the last day to breathe art
in progress in Mrs. Grant's room.

I dart into the art room
to finish cleaning out my drawer,
and decide to leave Mrs. Grant's gift
on her desk and run,
when she comes bustling in, all smiles.

"Laura, I was hoping you'd stop by. I was
going to mail this to you if I missed
seeing you today."

She holds the registration form
for the art contest so I can see it,
and goes through it
page by page,
making sure I understand all the parts
that need to be filled out.

The room feels too bright,
like the searing sunlight in Arles
must have felt penetrating Vincent's troubled brain,
or like Hopper's stark brightness

that floods his pictures with so much light
you have to keep blinking to let it in slowly.
Now the overhead fluorescents
and the sun streaming through tall windows
bear down on me hard,
washing out the perfect picture —
Mrs. Grant and me
getting ready to take the art contest
by storm. I rub my eyes
to tone it down,
to make the glare stop pulsing
off the glossy white paper.

Maybe it's because the sun is shining
Maybe it's because the sun is shining

Mrs. Grant folds up the form
and places it into my hands,
lingering for a moment with both her hands
on mine.

"Let me know, Laura, how you are doing
over the summer, will you?"

The smile has faded from her eyes
as she probes deep into mine.

"Sure thing, Mrs. Grant.
Have a great summer."

I stop by my usual spot on the bridge
still holding the registration form in my hand.
I know I am no good at physics
because I can't decide if the form

would get to the bottom of the canal quicker
if I wadded it up and tossed it over the edge,
or if I wadded it up and held it in my hand
while I tumbled
over the edge.

The sun bearing down on my head
makes my scalp tingle as if a bunch
of Medusa snakes are crawling all over it,
and I wonder if it feels anything like
Vincent's head must have felt
when he was close to sunstroke
from all those hours of painting
in the hot sun in Arles.
Maybe the sun made it impossible for him
to think straight, confused his thoughts
like mine are right now.

I back off the ledge,
registration form still in hand,
to begin the long hot summer
at home.

BEST FRIENDS

Beth puts Johnny Mathis on
her brother's record player,
and we sit in the boys' cluttered room
with the shades down,
listening to "Misty."
"We had a great year, you and I,
didn't we?" she says, all stretched out,

hands behind her head
in a dreamy pose.
"With your sensational art abilities
and my scientific genius,
we'll take the world
by storm one of these days."

"Yeah, right. Piece of cake."
Beth's self-confidence never ceases to amaze me.

"So, what are you going to do for an encore
after the pelicans?" Beth asks.

Why don't you take up painting again?
painting again?
take up painting again?
again?

In the darkened room
behind closed eyes
I take up the paint brush
and put it to the easel,
but just as it makes contact with
the canvas, it snaps in two.
Like a brittle twig,
the end snaps off,
splattering paint everywhere.
My eyes pop open to find Beth
staring at me.

"Huh, Laura, how can you top that?"
she says, staring at me curiously.

"Top what?"

"Your famous pelicans, silly. Where are
you today, never-never land? I asked
what you're going to do this summer
for the contest? The pressure's on,
you know. Now you have to match
or outdo it for the rest of your portfolio."

I could never get back to that
never get back
to that.
Never.

"Never, Beth. I could never
get back to . . .
never top that."

I close my eyes to shut out
the stunned look
on my best friend's face.

CONFIRMATION

It doesn't help
that this one time
Daddy decides to take his religion
so seriously.

I sit in my room
with waves of heart sickness
in place of the actual sickness
I lied about this morning,
the morning of my big

confirmation,
when I told him I was really sick,
way too sick to get out of bed,
that I had been throwing up
all night
with some violent flu-like stuff,
maybe even food poisoning,
and I was sure I had a fever.

He looked me square in the eye
and said, "You don't look sick to me.
Get up now and get ready."

Maybe I should have told him the real reasons,
the fears that Mother would break out
in Hail Marys,
fall to her knees and begin crossing herself,
or be seized with that incessant itching
from the nervous rash
all over her hands and neck,
or get up and wander out
during my speech.

Instead, I made it worse.
I blew the lid off
the anger and bitterness
boiling up inside me
all these weeks.

"Why is your stupid old religion
suddenly so important?
Why do you drop me off on Sundays
and never come with me?
What good is religion, anyway?

It doesn't seem to do anybody around
here any good.
I hate it
and
I hate you."

He closed the door
without a word.
I waited for him
to come storming back in,
letting loose with his own anger,
maybe swearing
and slamming around doors
like he does
when he's really had enough,

but he didn't.

Instead
he quietly opened the door again
a few minutes later,
set a box on the edge
of the desk,
and left
without a word.
Now a white, leather-bound copy
of the King James Version,
engraved in gold lettering,
Laura Ingrid Wahlberg,
glares at me defiantly
from the corner of my desk
where I set it
after the storm subsided,
a reminder

forever
of the day
I didn't get confirmed.

MUD PIES

Maybe it's a peace offering
or just to clear my head
or break out of my
self-imposed prison,
but whatever you want to call it,
I offer to water Daddy's petunias.

He looks over the top of the paper,
studies me hard.

"Don't flood them out, now."

I wince,
then marvel
at how we communicate
or don't.

The hose pulsing through my fingers
soothes my anger.
Mosquitoes buzz and tease
around my face,
and sweet petunia perfume
tickles my nose.
I stop well before a flood,
put the hose away,
and return for the weeds.

Weeds weren't part of the bargain,
but the smell of cool evening air,
damp soil,
and the way the setting sun slants
across my back
makes me kneel down
and begin digging
pulling
plucking
scratching

and remembering.

The hatefulness
that cluttered this day
seems to melt into the damp earth
and suddenly,
I remember digging in this very spot,
not for weeds,
but to make mud pies
a long time ago.

I remember how good
the slippery mixture felt
on my hands,
dipped in deep
up past my wrists,
letting the sticky substance
ooze through my fingers.
I remember hauling the hose over to this spot
to add more water,
like my mother added liquid
when she was mixing dough
to get just the right consistency.

A little soil,
a little more water.
Then I poured some of the goo
into old pie tins
or odd-shaped cans Mother had given me
to make pretend cakes, breads, and pies,
and I rolled some more of the goo
with an old wooden rolling pin
and used rusty cookie cutters to
make pretend cookies of all shapes.
Soon it would be time for lunch
and maybe a nap,
and I would leave my morning's work
on the woodshed steps
to bake in the afternoon sun.

Now in the cool June dusk
I sit on the top step
and let myself get worked up,
I mean really excited,
even happy-excited
for maybe the first time in weeks,
at the thought of getting up early
in the morning
to make

mud pies.

JULY 1963

GARDENING

I wake with a start
and the realization
that I slept through the night
without ghostly intruders.
This gives me enough courage to
fold up my easel
and slide it under the bed
along with a pile of paints, brushes, and canvases —
an act of housecleaning I had been putting off,
dreading, really,

and now
all of a sudden
it seems easy.
The contest registration form pokes out at me
from under the bed.
I give it a final shove with my foot
and dress quickly,
old shorts and a T-shirt that seem snugger than
last year.

I'm surprised when Mother asks
where I'm off to this early.

"Uh, just out in the yard. I thought
I might try some gardening this summer."

Her lack of curiosity
and my lack of certainty about what I'm really doing
end the conversation.

I start digging in the alley behind the shed

near one of the apricot trees.
Digging with bare hands, the loamy topsoil
soon turns to a gummy, gooey consistency —
clay-like, just what I was hoping for.

I scoop up a large clump and form it
into a ball, massaging it back and forth
between my two hands.
And then I hear it,
the sluggish sound of a heavy vehicle
grinding its way up the dirt road.
Still holding the oozing blob in my hands,
sweat rolling off my forehead,
I look up just in time to see
a large, green riding lawnmower
labeled "City of Crawford Hills"
idle noisily in the middle of the road,
blocking our driveway.

"Laura? Laura Wahlberg?" a voice calls
from the driver's seat.

I'm both horrified and elated to see
Dennis Martin staring me up and down
in obvious amusement.

"I didn't know you lived way up here
on this hill," he says.
I smile sheepishly
as he glances around at our tar-paper shed
and tiny clapboard house.

He focuses back on me.
"Hey, you're lookin' good, Laura,

for someone out playing in the dirt so
early in the morning."
I hope the glare of the sun
hides the deep blush I can feel
coming on.

"I didn't know you worked for the city, either."

Now he looks sheepish, as if he knows
how ridiculous it seems for the son of such wealth
to be toiling away in the heat of summer.

"My old man has a thing
about work ethic."
He shrugs apologetically and grins.
"Hey, listen, maybe we can get together
sometime this summer, now that I know
where you live."

Now that he knows that where I live
would fit into one room
of where he lives,
I won't count on it.

"I got a cool new ride
and a green light for passengers . . ."

"Somehow I knew that."

"Yeah? News gets around, doesn't it?"

"Sure does."

"Well, gotta split for now. I'll be

in touch."

Yeah, right.

He flashes his gorgeous smile and guns
the motor up the road.

I sit for a long time
tossing the dripping blob back and forth
from hand to hand.

Dennis

Martin

Dennis

Martin

Dennis

Martin

CAMP

I can't wait until next week when
Beth, Diane, Sandra, and I go to
Camp Ka-est-a on
Lake O' the Woods.
Daddy threatened to cancel
after I refused to go to the confirmation ceremony
until Aunt Hazel
made a rare phone call to him
saying fresh air would

do me a heap more good
than confirmation,
and he'd already paid for it
before all the hospital bills,
so he might as well let me go.

When Beth calls to check on my packing progress
I don't tell her my mother forgot
she had signed me up
even though I've gone every year
since fourth grade,
and that Grandma and Paula took
me shopping and tried to make light
of the fact that I didn't have any of the things I needed,
and here it was
two days before camp begins.
I don't tell her Mother's explanation —
that the shock treatments have taken away
her memory for a little while,
but it should get better in time.
I don't tell her how tempted I am
to forget to come home from camp
and leave all the forgetfulness behind.

I do tell her Dennis Martin
stopped in my driveway to tell me how fine
I looked covered in mud.

"What were you doing?" Beth asks.

"Well, I had planned on making mud pies . . ."

"Laura, girl, you are hopeless!"

SHOCK TREATMENTS

There is no listing in *Webster's Dictionary*
for shock treatment,
and few people
I care to ask.

Paula just brushes me off,
says they hooked Mother's head up
to a bunch of wires
and shocked the craziness right
out of her.
She'll be good as new in time.
Just give it more time.

Daddy says they did
whatever they had to do to help Mother
snap out of it. That's all
he cares about.

All I know is
that my own mother
can't remember
where we've been
or where we are going.

GLAD IT'S NOT ME

"I want to go home," Sandra wails.
"I hate it here. I want to go home now."
I try to get it out of her —
what's wrong,

did someone say something that upset her,
or does she not feel well?
Seemed like she had been excited about
coming to the camp I've talked so much about
since grade school.

I go to the counselor,
feeling a little embarrassed
that my fifteen-year-old cousin
is homesick,
if that's what it is.
The counselor looks straight at me.

"Do you know what's wrong?"

"All I can figure is that she misses her mom.
They are very close."

It takes my aunt a few hours to get here.
She's smiling and pleasant, gives me
a hug, and calmly settles Sandra
and her things into the car
without a question.

"Enjoy the rest of your week.
I'll tell your mom what a love you are."

As I wave at the cloud of red dust
retreating down the road,
I realize how mesmerized I am
by her sweet fragrance,
how good her hug felt,
and how un-close I am to
my mother.

CAMP CONVERSATIONS

"No offense, Laura,
but your cousin's a little weird,"
Beth says.

"Yeah," Diane chimes in. "I think
it was that conversation she had
with the girls in Cedar Tent. I heard
she tried to convince them
she talks to the Virgin Mary,
I mean, like, for real." She rolls
her eyes dramatically.

"Well, she does, but it's hard
to explain. Let's talk about something
else." They give me a strange look.
I check my watch and hope the dinner
bell rings soon.

"Well, how about your art? We haven't
seen you sketching down by the lake
like we usually do. Did you forget
your art stuff?" Beth asks.

"I'll bet you're working on something
really cool for the contest, huh?" Diane
jumps in excitedly.

My pulse starts racing.

I could never get back to that
never get back to that
back to that

never
get back to that

"Taking a break,
you know,
a breather,
need some new ideas,
you know?"

They nod
and totally don't know.

PATHETIC PINCH POT

I stop at the craft cabin
by myself after dinner
to admire a crude pinch pot
resting lopsided and uneven
on the top shelf.
I am amazed at how many steps
it took me
just to make
that simple little pot.

Yesterday the instructor plunked down
a lump of clay
about the size of a cantaloupe
under the nose of each of us
seated at a workbench.
I loved how it smelled like the earth,
like mushrooms in the forest after rain,
and how cool and smooth it felt

under my fingers
before I started kneading it.
I turned it in my hands,
folded it over and over
on itself until it started to warm up,
all the time working it,
pinching, pushing,
pulling, shaping,
sort of like making bread.

"You're pathetic."

I look around to see if anyone
is watching me giggle
and talk to a pot,

and I feel
like I have dug
deep down into the earth,
deep down into my soul
to discover an important piece of the puzzle

like an archaeologist
discovering a precious shard.

HOME AGAIN

Mother sets up the card table outside
under the apricot trees,
but the hot, dry air is so still
and the cicadas so loud,
grasshoppers everywhere,

it's hard to muster up
much of an appetite.

I chatter on and on about camp.
Daddy, his usual silent self,
looks up from his food only once,
stares straight into my face
to say he noticed
I left my art supplies behind.
My cheeks burn,
and I want to say
it's none of his business,
and why did he go through my room
while I was gone,
but I figure that would just start us up
where we left off
before camp,
and it's too hot, anyway.
I just shrug my shoulders.
He grunts, as if he got the answer
he expected.

Mother makes occasional comments
like she's really interested,
and I'm thinking maybe
I'll mention the craft cabin
when she says,

"Why didn't Sandra stay the week?"

"I think she missed her mother."

I ask to be excused.

It feels like the conversation
has moved too close to the fire,
and one of us
is sure to get burned.

FISHING

Daddy and I go fishing
Saturday morning up on Wood River.

The sun spreads across the valley
like butter on warm toast,
taking the chill
off the air between us.
Something about fishing —
maybe the routine,
choosing the right hook,
attaching the bait,
pointing the pole
toward the best dark hole,
or the rhythm,
casting, waiting, reeling,
casting, waiting, reeling —

something about fishing
loosens Daddy's tongue
better than his favorite beer.

I try to listen
when he gets going,
because I'm curious
how this man,

this quiet,
hard-to-understand
father of mine,
got so smart
never finishing high school,
going to work in a sawmill,
staying there all these years,
with probably no intention of ever
doing anything else with his life.
He knows the name
of every tree in the forest
and a whole lot of details
about growing conditions,
soil, disease, climate,
anything you want to know,
and from there he goes into poetry.
He knows a ton of
Edgar Guest poems by heart,
and he's always talking about
Joyce Kilmer's poem
"I think that I shall never see
a poem lovely as a tree."

I look for an opening to apologize
about confirmation,
but I hate to interrupt him —
and besides,
it feels like the warm sun
and the clear, crisp air
and the occasional splash of fish
in the icy cold river
have all but evaporated
the ill feelings between us.
Anyway, it requires all my concentration

getting the wiggly worm
on the hook,
casting into the water
without snagging on a bush.

And snagging on a bush
brings out the worst
in my father.

I wouldn't want to do that
today.

CERAMICS VERSUS POTTERY

"Whose idea was this, anyway?"
Beth asks, as we walk to town.
"I'm sure you could fry an egg
on this sidewalk today."

"C'mon, you know you want to unload
some babysitting money on a Beatles record,
and I need some clay."

"Do I dare ask what you plan to do
with the clay?"

I surprise myself
by going into great detail
about this new passion,
how it started
in Daddy's petunia bed,
and how it really got going at camp

when I discovered the craft cabin,
how it makes me feel
full of art again
in a whole new way.
My voice picks up speed
so she can't interrupt
by asking
one more time,
whatever happened to painting
and the art contest.

"It's all about touch
and movement," I say.
"I love how the texture
and temperature
change as you begin working
this blob of earth
with your fingers and hands.
You saw the two pinch pots
and three coil pots I made at camp,
and I've got this fantastic
idea for some figurines,
you know,
shapes of people, not pots."

"Isn't your mother into ceramics?" Beth asks.

I bristle.
"My mother's ceramics
and my pottery
are two entirely different things.
She paints something from a mold.
I create something from scratch."

"Oh, I see," says Beth.
I don't think she does.

But I do.

EASY FISHERMAN - FIGURINE # 1

He sits on a log

pole across his lap

baiting the hook

old felt hat

tipped slightly

toward one brow

cigarette dangling

from corner of mouth

lips curled with hint of a smile.

THE CALL

"He called. HE CALLED!"

"What? Stop shrieking. I can't understand you.
Speak clearly into the mouthpiece, madam.
Did you say someone is bald? Who is this, anyway?"

"Beth, stop playing with me, you dimwit. You know
who this is and what I said."

"So darling Dennis finally called. So?"
Beth is unable to hide her biased opinion.

I ignore her sarcasm and spend
the next half hour recounting the conversation,
how he mentioned how great it was to see me
digging in the mud at my house that day
before camp, how we're going in
his Riviera to a party at Suzanne Ditmar's home
on Lakefront Drive way out on the point
where the super big houses are,
how Howard is taking Megan
so we'll be double dating,
and how it's a poolside Hawaiian luau,
and how I can't believe this is happening,
and how it already makes me nervous enough
to throw up.

"Well," Beth says dryly. "I'd be throwing up
too, if I had to spend an evening with 88 Fingers
and his cheerleading pals.
Seriously, I can't believe
your father will let you go,

and even if he does,
you wouldn't really consider it,
would you?"

Of course I would.
Of course I can get around my father.
Of course Beth is just jealous.
Of course it's not exactly my crowd.
Of course I can manage the nerves
and the fact that Dennis will
        have to come to my house
        and meet my parents.

STUPID

Daddy said okay,
mostly because Mr. Ditmar
is vice-president of the mill,
and Daddy said it wouldn't hurt
Mr. Ditmar to see me there,
but I have to be home by eleven,
and he needs to meet Dennis.
Mother had little to say
other than, "Who is Megan?"
Megan, my friend since fifth grade,
who has the only house big enough
to hold all the Girl Scout dinners
we've ever had.

I hate it.
She can't remember anything.
It's as if she has been

absent from my life
for the last ten years.
Not only that,
but the medicine they put her on
turns her into an absolute zombie.
She's back to sitting and staring again,
just like before May.
Maybe she's getting ready
to do it all over again,
to go back into the Twilight Zone.

At the dinner table I said,
"It's really stupid,
the way you can't remember
who any of my friends are."

Daddy sent me away from the table
before I got a chance to tell him
I wasn't calling *her* stupid,
just the whole situation

STUPID
        STUPID
                STUPID.

AUGUST 1963

THE APRICOT TREE

The apricots hang like little golden
suns in a sea of billowy green.
They will be ready for eating and canning soon,
and that means this endless summer
is finally wearing down.

I climb up where two limbs
create a perfect U
and I slip in,
letting my body conform to the shape
of the sloping branches,
just the way I did
when I was a little girl.
The tree holds me
like a mother cradles a child,
and the soft rustle of the leaves
soothes like a mother's breathing,
in and out
in and out.
Mother sits across the yard
in the old beige rocker,
watching through a cloud of smoke.
Her listless body
moves with the chair,
back and forth
back and forth.

I let my mind drift with the swaying breeze
and carry me back to the magic evening
with Dennis, where the pool
shimmered in paper-lantern glow and
the slow dances melted me right into his arms,

and the beer,
yes, the first beer ever,
made it easy to forget about splotchy necks
and mothers who painted
themselves into a corner.

WOMAN AND TREE - FIGURINE #2

Blank-faced woman

rocking

smoking

beside a tree

ripe with fruit

and

a young climber.

DOG DAYS

I pick the pen up
and put the pen down,
but no matter how I write it,
red hot anger
burns a hole on the page
before I can finish a sentence.

I've lost track of how many hours
I've whiled away
trying to get off my chest
how angry I am at Beth.

Maybe it's just that point in the summer
that Grandma calls the dog days.
Nothing cools down the heat,
carefree turns into monotony,
best friends bicker
over nothing.

Well,
maybe more than nothing.
She may be my best friend,
but it's really none of Beth's business
whether I produce art
or not.

Maybe she meant well
telling me I'd regret
not going after the art contest.

But she had some nerve
telling me

I'd regret
hanging out with Dennis.
I never should have told her about the beer.

"Next thing you know
you'll be doing drugs, Laura."

She's just plain jealous, that's all.

COMMANDER IN CHIEF

It's canning day, and that means
Grandma takes charge of the kitchen.
I mean, she really takes over
like she lives here.
That drives Daddy up the wall,
so it's a good thing we do the canning
while he's at work.
Grandma's about half a head taller than Mother,
but she seems even taller
because she has this straight-back posture
that would really make points
with old Honeycut.
Last year in home ec
we had to walk around
with a pile of books on our heads
to check our posture.
I'll bet it would have been a piece of cake
for Grandma.

I don't know her as well as Paula does.
Paula told me Grandma practically raised her

when she and Mother had to live at Grandma's house
a long time ago.
Sometimes Grandma's kind of scary looking
with all that hair piled on top of her head,
more blue than grey,
and never a hair out of place.
She always wears a hairnet
when she's cooking, like today.

Mother tells me Grandma loved to hear me talk
when I was little.
But these days,
I can't ever think of much
to say to her.
I watch without a word as she
glides around the kitchen,
telling Mother and me
what needs to be done,
organizing the slicing, stirring,
boiling, sealing, and labeling
of the ripe apricots
into her famous
pineapple-apricot jam.
When I think it's safe enough to talk,
I ask, "Grandma, did you do the cooking
when you and Grandpa owned the hotel?"

"No, child, I oversaw the kitchen
and every other part of the business.
Lord knows your grandfather
was too far gone to give me any kind of help."

"What was he far gone with?" I ask.

Grandma pours paraffin onto the tops
of a row of jars to seal them.
Mother gives me a look like maybe
I had better do the same
with my lips.

"We don't know what ailed your grandfather.
His mind went, and we couldn't do much to
bring him out of it before he passed on."

A shiver travels down my spine.

How much does Mother
resemble
my grandfather?
How much do I
resemble
my grandfather?

GRANDFATHER - FIGURINE #3

Old blank-faced man

slouched in chair

head drooped down to one side

blanket-covered lap

hands palm down

resting on thighs.

GRANDMOTHER - FIGURINE #4

Tall stately woman

hair pulled back in bun

topped with hairnet

fashionable print dress

fastened at the V-neck

with a fancy brooch

mouth open

hand pointing

giving directions.

SECRET STASH

Every night lately
I sleep
and before I sleep
I peek
at the figurines

stashed on the top shelf
in the closet
behind my suitcase.

My new family.

SEPTEMBER 1963

FIRST DAY JITTERS

The first day of school
always hits me in my stomach,
where it feels like a swarm of butterflies
has taken up lodging.
Even after the longest summer on record
I dread this first day
of my junior year.
I can't decide if I should wear
the new long-sleeve brown plaid dress.
It'll probably be too hot
by this afternoon,
but the sweat circles under the armpits
would be less noticeable
than they would be
in the light blue dress.
But the light blue dress
would probably be cooler
when I sweat, which I'm sure I will do,
especially if I run into Dennis.

Mother calls me for breakfast,
which, of course,
I couldn't possibly eat,
and now I'm late anyway,
so I decide on the brown plaid
and then start messing with my hair,
which probably does look stringy
just like Uncle Ned says,
and the sweat is already starting
to stain my dress,
so I grab the sweater
and worry about how hot

it will be by this afternoon.

Now I really don't have time for breakfast
even if I was hungry,
so I fly out the door
hollering "Goodbye"
over my shoulder
and "Good riddance"
once I get out the door.

When we meet on the bridge
Beth looks cool as a cucumber
even with her new A-line plaid wool skirt
and matching sweater.
She didn't have as far to walk
as I did.

"Holy cow, you look hot,"
she says, and I know she's not commenting
on my ability to attract the opposite sex.
"You should take your sweater off
if you're that hot."

"I can't get my armpits to stop dripping,"
I say breathlessly.

"Just cool it, Laura. It's only the first
day of school. What could be so hard
about that? You know they just spend
all day getting everybody's screwy
schedule straightened out and handing
out the syllabus anyway."

"Yeah, right."

How's your mother, Laura?
How's your art, Laura?
How's your crazy mother, Laura?
How's your crazy art, Laura?

Art contest.
Mother
Art
Mother
Art
Mother

It's only the first day of school.

GHOST

I practically drop my lunch tray
when Mrs. Grant
seems to step
out of nowhere.

"Laura! How are you, darlin'?"

"Uh, fine, thanks, Mrs. Grant, and you?"

"I'm fine and will be even finer
when you fill me in about your portfolio
in class."

"Sure thing, Mrs. Grant. I'll see ya later."
I don't have the heart to tell her
she won't be seeing me in her class this year at all.

"You look like you've seen a ghost,"
Beth says with her mouth half full.
"Let me guess. You just saw *him*
coming to the convenient aid
of a cheerleading damsel in distress."

I take a deep breath and look Beth
square in the eye.
"Actually, he just asked me
if I wanted to do some drugs with him
this weekend, but . . ."

I bite into my sandwich
and try not to laugh at this rare moment
when my best friend
is finally rendered speechless.

I take pity on her and assure her
I'm only joking,
and I note how easily the subject of art
got lost in the transaction.

Score one for me.

LEAVE ME ALONE, WON'T YOU?

They won't leave me alone about it.
All week I've avoided Mrs. Grant,
Beth, Diane, Megan,
Daddy, Paula, Aunt Hazel,
other teachers,
everybody but Mother,

who doesn't seem to notice
or care.
Everybody keeps asking,
"Where's your sketch pad?"
"How's your portfolio
for the art contest coming?"
"Why aren't you interested
in art anymore?"

I wish they would all
leave me alone.
How could I ever explain
that painting drove my mother nuts,
stark raving mad?
I know
because I was there to see
what it did to her,
for goodness' sake,
and I'm sure it will
do the same to me
if I ever take up painting
or even sketching again.
I mean, we're in the same family.
In fact, that's probably where I got the gift.
Like Mrs. Grant says,
I've got the gift,
and let's face it,
Mother was pretty good
once upon a time,
enough to make me think
of Rembrandt sometimes,
so if I got the gift from her,
I must have her genes,
and I know from biology

that those genes are sitting there
inside me
ready to go haywire
just like hers.

So I tell Mrs. Grant I'm working on
some new ideas,
she'll be proud of me when she sees them,
and I'll be showing her soon.

I just leave out the true part,
that the registration form is somewhere
under my bed
buried in summer dust
along with paint supplies
and dreams of winning any contest
at all.

Besides,
I've got my "new family,"
but it's my secret for now,
my secret.

GOSSIP

Beth, Megan, and Diane
are seated in a tight cluster
at the lunch table,
so involved in a conversation
that my taking a seat
startles them.
They stop talking and all look at me

at the same time.

Are they talking about . . .
no, it couldn't be . . .
these are my best friends
but . . .

"Hi, everybody. Is
something wrong? Why
are you all looking at me
that way?"

I'm barely breathing.
It's about my mother.
I just know it is.
They are talking about her
and me
and her whole stupid situation,
maybe even the lie.
That's it.
They have put two
and two together,
and they know
I'm lying
about the blood disorder
and they are ready
to dump me
forever
for being a liar
as well as being crazy
just like her.

Giggles relieve the tension until
Megan pipes up with, "Laura has some

news, don't ya, Laur?"

I'm breathing again,
but shaking all over.

Before I can figure out where
this conversation is going,
Diane answers for me.
"Yes, she does! Howard told
me in Werner's class this morning
that Dennis . . ."

"Oh no, not another pool party,"
Beth interrupts.

". . . asked Laura to be his
campaign manager. He's running for
junior class president, you know.
Right, Laura?"

I blush and nod.

"Well, at least we know he'll have
high-quality campaign posters,
right, Laura?" Beth asks.

I shrug and nod.

There doesn't seem to be much
left for me to say
in this conversation.

CAMPAIGN MANAGER

I steady myself,
leaning over the poster
on the heated floor of Dennis's
three-car garage.
I clutch the dripping red paintbrush,
my lifeline.
If I let go for a second,
the anxiety brimming below the surface
will pull me down,
and I will drown
in a Jackson Pollock frenzy
of disorganized splatters.

Why am I here? I don't belong here.
How did I let myself get into this mess
in the first place?

The chatty din of cheerleader voices
echoes around me,
and the spray-paint fumes
floating in the closed space
threaten to bring up what little breakfast
I managed to eat.
I practically jump out of my skin
when a pair of feet stop next to me
and a hand gently lands on my shoulder.

"Laura, man, you are the greatest."
Dennis leans down and looks into
my eyes. "These posters are fab,
and hey, you look cute with red paint
on your nose."

He flashes the smile
and I start breathing again,
trying to gather my thoughts enough
to speak,
when he stands up,
responding to a female voice
crooning his name
across the garage.

Why am I here?

BIRTHDAY SHOPPING

On the Saturday before Mother's birthday
Daddy comes into my room
to wake me up
and quietly hands me some cash
to get a present.

"I have babysitting money,
you know," I tell him.

He would never admit it,
but I think he's afraid
I might just forget to get
her something without
his prompting.
It makes me sad
that he would think that
and sadder
that I would consider it —
not getting her anything.

I stash the wad in the side pocket
of my purse and head for the library
to meet Beth.

After we finish studying
we head for Woolworth's.
"Do you have any brilliant ideas
for a birthday gift for my mother?"
I ask her, sipping my cherry Coke.
I immediately regret bringing it
up because it will probably
get Beth going on a bunch of questions
I don't want to answer.

"You mean something here,
at the five-and-dime?"

I laugh. That's definitely not the question
I was expecting.

"Okay, wise guy,
you know my mother
is not my favorite person,
but, come on now,
I mean other stores."

"How about that new art store
over on 10th Street?
I think it's called Simone's.
I heard some artsy lady from San Francisco
has moved in with a bunch of
different kinds of art stuff. Your mom
is still into ceramics, isn't she?"

I flash a grateful smile at my
friend who has all the right answers.
"I knew I could count on you.
Wanna come?"

Beth says she has to get home,
so I head over there alone.

The shop is small
and airy and light,
more like an art gallery
than a gift store,
and it smells like clay or stone
or some part of the earth.
It is full of sculptures,
some placed in corners
on pedestal displays,
and some in the middle of a row
so you can walk around
and see the whole thing,
serious sculptures,
even nudes,
some just heads,
or busts I guess they call them,
and some just shapes,
swirling and curling and knotted
and twisted shapes
that leave it all up
to your imagination.
I don't see any price tags
or anything resembling cheap ceramics,
but I know for sure
I am in the wrong place,
so I turn to leave

and bump right into
the saleslady.

HALF PRICE

"May I help you find something?"
The lady I bumped into
stands out like an art piece herself
in a shift dress
full of helter-skelter bright colors,
dangly earrings,
and the most beautiful long, gray hair
I have ever seen.
She seems amused by the way we just collided.

I'm embarrassed to tell her
that I don't think I can afford
a single thing in her shop,
so I say, "No, thank you"
and turn toward the door.

"Wait," she says. "Did
you see this half-price rack
back here?"

I shake my head
but can't resist her friendly
invitation to take a peek.
I'm surprised to see smaller items
that I might be able to afford,
and then she steers me to
a little porcelain figurine

of Mary holding the Christ Child,
and she tells me the price
when she sees me eyeing it so long.
It's still more money than I have
by a few dollars,
but I can't take my eyes off it
because it really seems like
something my mother would like,
and I stare at the saleslady curiously
because I wonder how she knows
it might be just what I'm after
when I haven't even told her
who I'm shopping for
or what they might like.

"Uh, it's nice, really nice,
sort of what I'm looking for,
but I don't have enough money."

She says she's a good judge of
character, and she can tell I'm honest,
and she is willing to give
me the piece now, and I can bring
her the difference
whenever I get it.

I am speechless.
I just stare at her
while she carefully wraps it.
Without seeming to probe,
she finds out it's for
my mom,
even gift wraps it,
and says she's sure my mom

will love it,
and whenever I can get back
with the rest of the money
is fine with her.

"By the way,
you seem interested in art, too.
Are you?" she asks.

I'm halfway out the door.
I pretend I don't hear her
because I feel
as transparent as glass.

POSTERS, SLOGANS

I rummage quickly under my bed for paint,
as if the troll under the bridge
will grab my hand and pull me under
if I'm not careful.

I spread out on the floor without the easel
and churn out the last of the posters.
Easy little slogans, cute sketches.
Nothing serious, keeping it light
and easy.

I stand back and look at the work,
the work I did for Dennis,
whom I've barely seen in the past two weeks
because he's been so busy with his campaign —
that's really it,

he's just been too busy to hardly talk at all.
I survey the posters, slogans,
catchy phrases, loud colors,
broad, brush-stroked letters,
signs on sticks,
and see them
for what they are.

This is as far as it goes.
I could never get back to that
I could never get back to that
I could never, never get back to that

I quickly clean the brushes,
slide them under my bed again,
climb up to the top shelf
of my closet,
and pull out the clay family.

This is where I really belong now.
This is where I live.

CONFIDENCE

Beth catches up with me
just outside English class,
and I'm bursting to tell her about
the shopping trip to Simone's,
but she wants to talk about the
assignment we just got,
the one that leaves me feeling
like I just took a punch in the stomach.

Even thinking about
getting up in front of the class
does that to me.
It doesn't bother Beth in the least.
I wish I could be like her.

"So, you must be excited," Beth says.
"Your dad's an expert
on poetry. I'll bet he'll be able to give
you some great pointers."

"Excited is not exactly the word
I'd use to describe discussing my favorite poem,
let alone reciting it by memory,
in front of all those Tremont creeps.
And my dad is hardly an expert,
he just happens to know
a lot of poems by heart,
and I'd rather not talk about it
right now anyway
if you don't mind."

One thing about Beth is
she can take a hint,
so she drops the poetry talk and asks about
my trip to Simone's.

The knot in my stomach unravels
as I describe the way it went,
how nice the saleslady was
and how fancy and beautiful
all the art pieces were,
even if they were way out of my price range,
and how I'm going to pay her back

with babysitting money
as soon as I can.

"Speaking of babysitting," Beth says,
"I recommended you to the Gerards."

She tells me her regular sitting job for the Barlows
keeps her way too busy,
and it's too fun nosing around
their geodesic dome
with that spectacular view,
and she likes the free time she has
when their one kid takes his nap,
so she doesn't have time anymore
to sit for Mrs. Gerard,
the nutcase drama teacher
with the two bratty kids
and all the far-out paintings
all over her house.

"Gee thanks, Beth.
You're a true
blue friend today."

By now I'm laughing at this
outrageous best friend
with all the self-confidence
you'd ever need in life,
and I'm maybe even laughing
at myself,
because God knows,
I ought to be able to
handle a nutcase
better than most.

MISSING

I spend the walk home thinking about Dennis,
how quiet he's been since he lost the election
by a hair to his best friend, Howard.
Beth, Diane, and Megan have bets going
about whether he'll ever ask me out again
now that the campaign is over.
I don't care what they say,
he still chose to sit by me
in English class.

My thoughts quickly evaporate
and my heart lurches when
I spot Paula's car in the driveway
and hear her yelling at Kim and Jeff
to get out of the backseat of the car
right this minute before they get a spanking.
Daddy is standing in the doorway,
home way too early.
Something is wrong.

"Mom is missing,"
Paula says breathlessly before
I can even ask. Her cheeks are flushed.
"Aunt Hazel didn't get an answer
to her usual morning phone call,
so she called me. I've been out
driving around, looking for her,
going to places I think she might go,
and nothing, nothing at all,
so we've called the police."

Paula sits down, fanning herself,

and starts crying like I've never
seen her cry before,
and then Jeff starts wailing,
like he does when he wants
something in the grocery store
that he can't have,
and I pick him up and try to calm him
so Paula can get herself together.
Daddy heads out to the shed
and slams the back door on the way,
and then Kim says she feels
like she's going to throw up.
I'm starting to feel like the only
healthy one in the house
because I don't feel like crying
or throwing up,
which really surprises me,
but I figure it must be
because I'm just too shocked
to have any kind of reaction,
and then I start having really
crazy thoughts,
like maybe Mother's running an errand
or shopping
or visiting a friend,
and the reason I know these
are crazy thoughts
is that she doesn't have any friends,
and she hasn't run any errands
or done any shopping
or gone anywhere
beyond the backyard
on her own
since way before last May.

OKAY

I guess you could call it a
false alarm.

The police find Mother just before dark
down at the canal,
unable to tell them her name.
Funny thing is
she wasn't far from where I stopped
once
to think about basic colors.

Dr. Goodman is able to meet her at his office
right away when they call him, and he says
she took too many pills
by accident
and it made her a little out of it
for a while —
forgetful,
disoriented,
confused,
but not the usual
over-the-top crazy.
She should be back to normal,
whatever that means,
by morning.
She doesn't have to go away
to the hospital this time.
He says just keep an eye on her tonight
and make sure she takes
all her medicine correctly
in the morning.

I never thought
I would be disappointed
when Dr. Goodman says,
"She's okay,"
and sends her back home.

LEANING OVER THE EDGE - FIGURINE #5

A female figure

on a bridge

both hands on railing

right foot resting

on the middle slat

left foot on tiptoe

ready to swing up

over and down.

OCTOBER 1963

POETRY IN MOTION

The stupid poem assignment is due
in two days, and here I haven't even
found a stupid favorite poem yet,
let alone started to memorize it.
There's just been too much going on,
and I just might have to tell the teacher
I'm not ready for class
day after tomorrow.
Or I could just be sick —
maybe that's best,
to just be sick.
I'm actually getting pretty good
at being sick.

Daddy pulls out his thick copy
of *Collected Verse of Edgar A. Guest*,
his all-time favorite,
and he turns to some of them
that have ragged pieces of paper
marking the page,
and he starts reading them out loud
to give me some ideas.
There is one called
"The Dreamer" that's
kind of catchy,
but then I get sidetracked
when a pile of newspaper clippings,
all brown and tattered-looking,
fall out of the back of the book.
Daddy looks a little startled,
clears his throat,
and says they are the poems she sent to him

when he was stationed in North Africa.

Now I'm confused, because I always
thought he was the one who
originally sent the poems to her,
but maybe it was the other way
around. Anyway, I get
embarrassed when he starts
showing them to me
because some of them
are downright mushy,
even racy and passionate.
I'm thinking he's probably
made some mistake and gotten
an old girlfriend's stuff
mixed up with my mother's stuff
because this certainly isn't the mother
I know.
If this is my "old" mother,
I want to know more about her.
I already know more than I want to know
about this "new" mother.

I'm just sure someone,
somebody I know,
probably saw her standing by the bridge
or worse yet,
saw them put her into the police car
when they found her the other day,
and I don't know how on earth
I can stand up in front
of that class and recite this poem
when my absolutely crazy mother
just took a ride home

in a police car
because she couldn't remember
who or where she was.

"Daddy," I say, "I'm going to bed.
I really don't feel well."

He almost looks relieved.

FOREST FIRE

The air carries the stench
to our door. The fire
is just ten miles west of here,
bad enough to close
the mill so Daddy
and his crew could help
fight it. The only good thing about it
is they also sent us home from school
early, and I didn't have to give my
poem recitation today.
Maybe the teacher will forget about it
altogether by next week,
although the one I picked
about the dreamer
wasn't so bad when I was doing it in front
of the mirror.
I wish it would be the same
in front of the class,
but it never is.

I can't sit out on the front porch,

the air is so bad.
I can't even see the mountains,
and the sky is a sick-looking mixture
of gray with a reddish glow toward the west.
Mother's back to pacing again,
and the fire has her all worked up.
The last thing Daddy said
was to call Paula
if anything happens
while he's gone.

It feels like there isn't enough air
in our house for both of us
to keep breathing.
The thought of being trapped
alone
with a crazy mother
in this suffocating night
makes me gasp for breath.

QUIET NIGHT

My head feels like
spaghetti. Daddy is still gone
and Mother hasn't slept
for two wild-eyed nights,
so neither have I.
Seems to me that Daddy
could have arranged for
Aunt Hazel or Paula
to look after Mother.

Paula finally took her to
Dr. Goodman today.
He gave her
more pills
to help her sleep.

I wonder if anyone would notice
if I took a few of them,
just one or two.

On top of everything else,
Mrs. Grant cornered me in the hall
today after sixth period.

"I'm sorry you're not in my class this year,
Laura. But I know you are working
hard on the contest portfolio.
I know you haven't forgotten that
the art submissions are due in January.
Is there anything
I can help you with? You know, the mailing
and packaging details and all?"

Her eyes search mine.
I don't hold her gaze long before looking down.
"No, but thanks anyway, Mrs. Grant."

I study Mother's medicine bottle for what
seems like hours
before deciding against it.
Maybe sheer exhaustion will be enough
to scare the ghosts away tonight.

WOMAN AND EASEL - FIGURINE #6

Middle-aged woman

wearing paint smock

smiling

easel under one arm

paint box in other hand.

FAINTING SPELL

Crawford Hills Hospital
has a free vaccine clinic,
and Paula says since she is
taking Kim and Jeff,
I should come along, too,
and get my polio shot.

"Paula, can I ask you something?"
The kids are quiet in the backseat
for a change.
It's a rare opportunity to talk.

"Sure, as long as I don't have to
think. I'm way too tired."

"Did you ever see all those love
poems Mother sent Daddy
during the war? Man,
she was a different person then,
wasn't she? How'd she get to be
so different,
so far away,
so distant,
like she's not here half the time?"

Paula looks across the front seat
so long, I'm afraid she's going to
lose control of the car.
She's flushed and she's angry.

"You'd be out of it, too, if you
had to take all the pills she does.

Let's drop it, okay?"

As if the car conversation isn't enough,
the hospital lobby is way, way too hot,
and waves of nausea hit me
as soon as I get inside the smelly,
crowded waiting room.
Within minutes,
I faint.

Dr. Goodman happens
to be on duty,
and he pulls me into
an exam room when
I come to.

He checks my vitals
and sits me on the edge
of the table.

"You doing all right?" he asks,
looking squarely at me with
his kindly, smiling eyes.

"Sure," I say.
I'm both embarrassed and puzzled.
He knows I just fainted
and that it's no big deal.
Besides, he's the doctor.
Shouldn't he be able to tell
if I'm doing all right?

"Listen. If there is ever anything
I can do to help you in any way,

I want you to let me know.
Do you hear what I'm saying?"

I nod, unsure what to do
with what he is saying.

RECITATION

I have the usual
racing heart
sweaty hands
cotton-ball mouth,
but it doesn't matter

because Dennis gives me a thumbs up
and an admiring smile
as I sit down
after my recitation of
"The Dreamer."

I'm caught completely off guard
when he rushes to catch me
going out the door.

"The poem, Laura, about the dreamer —
where'd you get it?"

My heart lurches. This is the Dennis
I saw at Megan's party, who pummeled me
with questions, deep questions,
about me
and where I come from

because
he really seemed to care.

“Oh, my dad collects poems by Edgar Guest.
A bit sentimental, but . . .”

“It’s you, Laura. I see why you like it. It fits.
You’re the dreamer, aren’t you?”

My blush approaches danger zone red
as I stand with my mouth wide open.
He listened.
He listened enough to consider
and think
and question.

I wonder,
does any of that translate into caring?

NEW PASTOR

Carla Upton comes right up to me after English class
today and introduces herself.
I already knew who she was
because Diane pointed her out.
Carla’s dad is the new pastor at Crawford Lutheran.

She invites me to join the new youth group.
She says the meeting will be
in the basement of the parsonage
on Friday night,
and the topic will be

"What I Want Out of a Youth Group,"
since there hasn't been one in such a long time.
"Do you know anything about
the spiritual gifts?"
she asks, totally switching subjects.

I must have a dumb look on my face
because I have no idea what she's talking about,
but she just keeps smiling
and says to come on over around six
for pizza and be prepared,
because her dad usually gets pretty jazzed up
when he's talking about miracles
and healing, stuff like that.

"I thought you said you were just going
to be organizing the youth group."

"Yeah, that for sure. But we just moved
here from Seattle, and there's lots
going on in the churches up there that isn't,
I mean, that hasn't made it down here yet.
Just come.
I promise it won't be scary."

Her eager smile wins me over, and I agree to come.

I tell Daddy about the meeting,
but leave out the part about miracles and healing
because it would probably throw him off
like it threw me off. I mean,
the last thing we need around here
is another Holy-Roller church like the
one our neighbors next door go to

where people yell and scream and
carry on like maniacs. That is definitely
not the way Lutherans do it,
in these parts, anyway.

"About time they got
something going there
for you teenagers," Daddy says
after I tell him about the new youth group.

I want to come back
with an "about time"
comment of my own,
but before I can, he surprises me
and says he'll go with me on Sunday
to check out Pastor Upton.

I know Mrs. Samuels,
my Sunday school teacher,
will be happy.
She can finally ask him to his face
why he drops me off
all the time and leaves.

I wonder myself
what goes on inside Daddy's heart.
He never lets on
how he feels
about all the junk with my mother —
well, maybe just that one time
when he started crying before we
went to see her in the hospital —
but he sure seems
to love her.

I suppose if our church
had confession like the Catholics,
I'd be there all the time
confessing how I don't
love my mother.

I hope we
don't talk about confession
at this meeting.

BABYSITTING JOB

When Mrs. Gerard finally calls to ask if I can
babysit, I try not to sound so eager,
but I quickly say, "Yes, anytime,"
because I am anxious to get that debt paid off
and, to tell the truth,
to have an excuse to browse
in Simone's again.
Mrs. Gerard says her husband will pick
me up on Saturday at six thirty sharp.
Brent and Tina will be ready for bed,
and all I need to do is a story,
a snack,
and off to bed they go
for seventy-five cents an hour —
and by the way,
I come highly recommended
by Beth, who says such nice things
about me.

"Thanks. I'm looking forward

to meeting you."

You should hear what Beth
has to say about you.

DIFFERENT KIND OF CRAZY

I'm only inside the door about fifteen minutes
before I begin to see what Beth
was talking about.

Brent pushes bedtime to the limit
after I tell him three times
in a very nice voice,
don't jump on the couch,
but he keeps telling me
he has to get his energy out and
he doesn't want to stop.

Tina is quiet enough,
but she stares at me a lot
and asks questions like
do I ever have stage fright,
and would I like to be an understudy?

I guess she's just a very peculiar child,
a drama teacher's child,
with a bunch of drama terms
rolling around in her head.
I finally bargain with Brent,
and agree not to tear down
the chair-and-blanket fort

in the family room,
and promise to make up a unicorn-and-dragon
story if he'll get in bed.

When it's quiet upstairs
I put Henry Mancini on the stereo
and do the usual wandering around.
I guess it's really more like snooping
or casing the joint, checking out this
ultra-modern two-story
in the Tremont district.

Mrs. Gerard's splashy, angular painting
over the fireplace
makes me blush, as if I am peeking
at something forbidden.
Beth had warned me her work
was plastered all over the house.
I can't tell if
it's supposed to be a flower part
or a body part, but it looks like something
that would cause snickers
from certain male students like Jerry Pruner,
maybe even Dennis.
Another one,
tall and full of bright colors,
fits the space perfectly over the stairs,
and looks sort of like someone set fire
to a shed or old building,
and you can almost feel the heat.

On the shelves next to the fireplace
sit some big-name classics —
Maugham, Hemingway,

Fitzgerald, Frost, Dickens,
Browning, Yeats —
and sitting face up
on the coffee table is a copy
of *A Farewell to Arms*,
with a place held about halfway through.

"Moon River" clicks off, and I sit
in the dim, hushed living room
with two wild kids upstairs
and a bunch of outrageous paintings
scattered all about,
and feel perfectly comfortable

in this house Beth calls
nutty.

SETTLING THE ACCOUNT

The most amazing thing . . .
I take the money I owe to Simone's
and it turns out
the saleslady is also the owner.

Her name is weird, spelled B-o-u-c-h-e-r,
but you say it *boo-shay*.
She asks me, again,
if I'm an artist.
No.
She puts it this way:
"What kind of art are you interested in?"

She's so direct,
so open about things without being pushy,
there is something about her that makes me
want to be direct, too
and to tell the truth.

So I tell her I used to paint,
but now I'm experimenting with clay.
That's the truth as near as I can
put it right now.

At the word *clay,*
her intense blue-green eyes
lock onto mine like a vise,
hold me in their gaze
for an eternity of seconds,
landing on

something, someone

elsewhere

sending shivers to my toes.

"Bring your work," she says.
"Bring it on Saturday
before the shop opens."

She's back with me now,
but I wonder where she flew off to
just seconds ago.

THE BACK ROOM

I stuff a few books in the bottom of the book bag
so it looks like I'm heading for the library.
Just in case Mother bothers to care
or wonder where I'm going,
I can tell her I'm going to the library,
as usual, to study with Beth,
because I just don't want her to know
what I'm up to. It's like a magical spell
will be broken if anyone finds
out what I'm doing right now,
especially her.
Then, one by one,
I take down the clay figurines
from the closet shelf
and carefully wrap each of the six pieces
in the newspapers I've been saving
from the pile out on the coffee table,
and I pack and unpack the bag
several times until I'm sure
the figurines won't slip down
and get smashed by one of the books.
It turns out I wasted my time with the books.
Mother, sitting slouched over coffee and a cigarette,
seems to have trouble focusing on me
and my well-planned lie.

Mrs. Boucher meets me at the door,
wearing a paint smock
scattered with clay smudges and a smile
so big it makes me a little nervous.
For a split second
I feel like I've made a mistake

coming here.

"Now then, sit down right here, dear, and tell me
all about yourself." She pushes
a plate of fancy pastries my way
and offers a glass of juice.

It's overwhelming,
having her complete attention
and the open invitation to talk
about me
in this shop full of expensive artwork
with my humble figurines
scattered on the table
between us.

My face starts turning red,
and my armpits get damp,
and, oh darn, this isn't an oral report
I'm giving, so why can't I just cool it,
like Beth would say,
but all I can do is stammer and stop.

She rescues me.

"You remind me of my daughter,"
she says, a rush of pink now
spreading across *her* silky cheeks.
I take a sip of juice to try and settle down,
and for a minute
I think she might actually start crying.

"She had hair like yours,
sweet smile, and eyes,

eyes that sparkled so
when she was happily occupied."
Mrs. Boucher walks across the room,
returns with a picture
of a girl intently working with clay,
hair falling down over both her shoulders.

She describes how confusing
it was when her daughter first started
showing signs that something was wrong,
how hard it was to sort out the early symptoms.
Was it just a bout of clumsiness, possibly a learning
disability, vision problems, seizures?
"It was a guessing game," she says.

"After many tests and a long period
of just watching the symptoms, they finally
landed on a diagnosis.
It's called Batten disease.
Before she was much older
than you, her body and her mind
began failing rapidly. She left us
when she was eighteen, the day
her class graduated from high school."

"I'm so sorry, Mrs. Boucher."

She goes on to answer a question
already forming in my head.
Her husband,
devastated by the loss of their only child,
suffered a complete mental
collapse, never fully recovering.
He died in a mental institution

two years ago.

“Mental collapse, is that
like a nervous breakdown?” I ask,
finally finding my voice,
even talking with my mouth half full.

She looks directly into my eyes.
“Yes, exactly.”

Now I’m ready to talk, and suddenly
I can’t get it out fast enough,
everything about Mother’s illness,
the weeks and months of craziness leading up to
the hospital, and how she came home so different,
but the weirdness continues now with
forgetfulness and zombieness and wandering off,
and how much I hate it
and even her
and how embarrassed and angry and sad I feel
and how I have lied to my friends
and now I worry that they will catch me in the lie
and how I’m afraid to draw or paint because
it might all happen to me,
but then I discovered pottery
and how good it feels,
like it’s the only good thing in my life right now,
well, maybe.
Mrs. Boucher leans back,
sighs deeply,
takes both my hands in hers
and says, “Well, Laura,
it looks like we are in this
together. Do you know why?”

"No . . . no, I really don't," I say,
giving her a completely honest answer
and a very blank stare.

"Well, it sounds like
we both have work to do,
and we can do it right here in
my shop, together."

She tells me how much joy
working with clay gave her
daughter. She says she can sense
that same joy reflected
in my figurines.

"And it would give me joy
if you would come and use this back room
anytime you want,
to pursue the wonderful work
you have begun. Ah, I see the first
customer waiting outside the door.
I'm open until six weekdays and until
three on Saturdays. I'll be glad
to see you, anytime."

She leaves me sitting
in a daze.
I quietly slip out while she waits
on the customer,
and when I'm halfway up the hill
I realize the clay family
has found a new home.

WHAT DOES SHE MEAN?

It sounds like we both have work to do
work to do
we both have work to do

I'm home from school, sick,
and Mrs. Boucher's voice
haunts me,
in and out of feverish dreams
so clear I could swear
she stood by my bed
with a glass of water
yesterday.

I can't get it out of my mind,
how good it felt to tell her
everything
when I saw her last week,
but now
every time I replay
that conversation in my head
I feel empty and angry
and confused.

Did I tell her too much?
Did she tell me too much,
or maybe
more than I wanted to hear?

we both have work to do

Is the clay family the only work
I have to do,

or did Mrs. Boucher
have something more
in mind?

NOVEMBER 1963

SAD NOTE, MAD NOTE

Dennis passes me a note in English class.
"Why so sad?"

Sad?
On top of everything with my family,
I've been out for a week
with strep throat, and I feel like crap.
If he really wanted to know,
he could have asked Diane or Beth.

My reply: "I've been out sick,
in case you haven't noticed."

He answers back. "Why don't you
paint a picture? That always used
to make you happy."

could never get back to that
work to do
could never get back to that
work
to
do

And then frustration —
futile, helpless, senseless frustration —
begins rising from my toes
all the way to the top of my pulsing head.
I pull my hair down around my face
and bury my head in the book so the teacher
doesn't choose this moment to call on me.

Waves of seething anger
at two-faced Dennis Martin roll over me.
Laughable, lovable, sweet-talking Dennis,
who goes out of his way to pretend to care
about people,
doesn't even notice
when the seat next to him goes empty
for days, and then he thinks he knows
what will make me happy
when he doesn't bother
to know me at all.

He obviously doesn't give a hangnail
about me.

OR DOES HE?

I hurry out the classroom door
as soon as the bell rings,
successfully avoiding Dennis's eyes.
I head straight for the nearest bathroom
where, inside the empty stall,
I try to muffle the sobs,
blubbering to an alarmed voice
somewhere in the bathroom
that everything is fine.

I let the tears run their course,
and as my nose-blowing sniffles die down,
I read the graffiti on the walls.

Brian is a cockroach

Marilyn was here
Your mama stinks
Girl you are messed up

The last lines get to me,
and I want to start crying
all over again
when it dawns on me.

I'm the one
who is here
with the messed-up problem.
I am the work
that needs to be done.

I dig into my book bag
for pencil and paper.

Dennis,
I'm sorry.
Thank you for caring.
Laura

I just have time
to slip it into his locker
before next class.

FRIDAY, NOVEMBER 22, 10:30 A.M.

The band room buzzes with chatter,
like it usually does
before the teacher comes in.

A student in the front row
nearest the PA system hears it first.
She stands up and points to the speaker,
shushing us with wild arm motions.
"The president," she gasps,
and now the announcement
is being repeated while the teacher
walks in quietly and stops in his tracks.
The room is dead still
when the principal's voice
comes through, slower this time,
leaning on every word:
"President John F. Kennedy has been shot."

The room erupts in gasps, some students
look like they are going to cry,
but mostly we are all shocked
that something like this could ever happen,
and we can hardly believe it when the principal
says to proceed in an orderly fashion
directly to our lockers,
right there in the middle of third period,
get everything we might need
for a long weekend since there
may not be school on Monday.

Everyone looks kind of dazed,
and the last thing we hear
is stay tuned to the radio for the updates
about school,
and get home safely,
that we need to be with family
at a time like this.
Everyone seems eager

to be headed home,

everyone but me.

FEARFUL

Diane, Beth, and I meet at the lockers
and walk out together.
Our breath forms little puffy clouds
as our nervous chatter hits the cold, crisp air.
On any other day, bets on the first
snow might have been the talk.

Is he alive?
Is he dead?
How did it happen?
Who did it?

Everyone is anxious to get home,
turn on the TV, and get the details
that have so interrupted
our morning, our lives.

I picture Beth walking into the warmth
of her cluttered house, Mrs. Watson
checking on something sweet baking
in the oven before sitting down
in front of the TV with an unfinished
sewing project in her lap.

I imagine Diane's mom, her planning
for the Girl Scout banquet

or her progress on one of Diane's
newest outfits interrupted
while she tunes in the TV.

I wish I could follow either of them
to their homes that won't threaten to implode
under the weight of such terrible news.

I'm anxious
about how much tragedy
our family,
my mother,
can absorb.

TV VIGIL

I can hear the TV before I even open
the door. It's turned up way too loud.
Mother sits in the rocker,
clutching her pink rosary,
with eyes glued to the screen
when I walk in.
Icy anxiety tightens
the muscles in my neck.

"I thought they'd send you home,"
she says in a far-away voice, without
taking her eyes off the screen.
"He's gone.
They just gave him last rites."

I drop my books

and focus on Walter Cronkite's
cracking voice. He looks and sounds
like he's going to cry, break down
right there in front of the whole world.
We sit in stunned silence
as a doctor from Parkland Memorial Hospital
recounts the details,
the angle of the bullets from the second story of the
Texas School Book Depository building
along the parade route
where Kennedy's motorcade passed by,
the chaos and confusion
to try to save him,
the time of arrival at the hospital,
and the exact pronouncement of death.

Mother smokes and rocks,
and together we watch the unfolding horror
replayed over and over
throughout the afternoon —
a smiling, waving president
in the Dallas motorcade
minutes before the shooting,
the Secret Service agent jumping
into Kennedy's limo
after the first shot,
Jackie's blood-splattered suit.

I steal glances at Mother's face,
watching for wild-eyed mania,
waiting for her to jump up and start pacing,
listening for the muttering to start,
the short circuits and disconnects,
expecting the national tragedy

to climb right through the screen
into our living room,
setting off an uncontrollable
chain of events.

Somehow
the afternoon passes
without incident.

KEEPING THINGS NORMAL

The assassination of our president
is what it finally takes to get Daddy to church.
So we go together on Sunday,
where we sing "Faith of Our Fathers"
and watch Pastor Upton break down
during a sermon focused on Kennedy,
and then we pick up Grandma for dinner.
Daddy says we're trying to keep things normal
on this long, sad weekend
unlike any I've ever known.

I think about *normal*
as we cross the viaduct and drive
out to the Catholic rectory
where Grandma keeps house
for the priests. I'm not even sure
what normal is when it comes to our
family. I want to flood the car
with questions about normalcy.
How do you keep things normal
in a household where

craziness is as common as
fruit flies in summer?
What if my mother breaks again
under the strain of so much sorrow
until there is no normal to get back to?
Do we have a plan,
any more than President Johnson has
a plan as he takes over being president —
and if so,
what is it?

All this I want to ask Daddy,
but I'm trying to keep things *normal*,
and all these questions probably wouldn't make
a very normal conversation.

SUNDAY DINNER

The first thing out of Grandma's mouth
when her heavy frame sinks
into the front seat
is, "How's Iris? I'll bet she's
worrying herself sick again
watching all the news."

"She's okay," I say, knowing
Daddy won't give Grandma the time of day.
For as long as I can remember,
there's been bad blood between these two.

Mother once told me
that Grandma made a comment

about Daddy being Norwegian.
He took it the wrong way,
even though she meant no harm.
He's awfully proud
of his Norwegian heritage, and he thought
she was putting him down.

Paula once told me Grandma said
Daddy ought to be ashamed of himself
the way he refuses to become a Catholic
so we could all go to the same church.

I overheard Daddy tell Mother once
that Grandma should stick to taking care of priests
and stop trying to take care of him.

Probably, if the truth be known,
only God has
the solution to this problem.

Now I hear the concern
behind Grandma's comment
that her daughter, my mother,
might worry herself sick again.
Breakdown scenarios play in my head
like the recent news coverage,
flashing from one traumatic snapshot to the next.

We head back over the viaduct
in silence, the long day
stretched out before us
like an obstacle course.

THE FUNERAL

The fuzzy murmur of TV voices
wakes me up. My room
isn't dark like it usually is
on a school morning,
and my heart starts pounding,
thinking I've overslept,
when I remember
we are in the middle of a
national crisis.

They've cancelled school today,
meaning I could stay in bed
or attend the funeral
now playing in our living room.
I want to stay in bed, but I can't ignore
the sounds on the other side of my bedroom wall,
Mother's rocker keeping time with
"Hail to the Chief" as Kennedy's coffin
travels to its final destination.

Outside my window the bare, wispy birch limbs
sway in the cold November wind.
The sky is as gray
as my unworked clay.

THANKSGIVING

Grandma, in her best silk dress
and the brooch I gave her for Christmas last year,
sits in Mother's rocker,

content with the thick *Herald and News*
special holiday edition.
Daddy managed to pick her up without
incident, or at least,
when they came in the door there was no evidence
of words between the two of them. It's probably
because he's hoping to slip down to the VFW
before we eat to have his little holiday drink,
and if he gets into it with Grandma,
Mother will be upset and make a fuss
about his going down there. If he stays
on her good side,
she doesn't seem to mind, as long
as he gets back in time to eat with us.

I stuff celery with pimento cheese
and plot the artistic arrangement
it will make on the Fostoria dish
along with olives, pickles, and carrots.
That's always been my job on Thanksgiving Day
since I can remember, to do the relish dish.
And then I'll mash the potatoes
and whip them with the electric mixer.
I stand at the kitchen window so I can
look out at the crusty snow
sparkling like diamonds
in the brilliant sun.
I think about how it was just
six days ago, during the long
Kennedy assassination weekend, when I could have sworn
the snow would come down looking gray
like everything else looked then,
and I was bracing myself
for another bout of craziness with Mother.

But today she got up early to put the turkey in,
and she's been busy all morning, looking and sounding
like, well, I really don't want to even say the word "normal"
because it's like it might break the spell,
but the house has all
the right smells —
roasted turkey,
sweet candied yams, mincemeat pie,
cloverleaf rolls,
giblet gravy.
I've been here in the kitchen with her most
of the time, and I haven't seen or heard
any craziness. She even said she was
looking forward to filling her plate.
I helped clean the house to get ready
for Paula and Frank and the kids,
who will be here any minute
with a carload of side dishes,
noisy toys, and lively chatter.

Maybe that's the secret. Keeping
her so busy she doesn't have time
to sit in that rocker and
worry
worry
worry
herself into craziness.

Whatever the secret is,
it's hard
not to be thankful today.

DECEMBER 1963

UNCLE NED'S NEW CAR

I'm getting ready to escape the madhouse
and meet Beth at the library
when Uncle Ned drops in
to show us his
shiny new red Buick LeSabre
four-door sedan,
an early Christmas present
he and Aunt Hazel bought for themselves.
He's pretty drunk for this early
on a Saturday morning.
Aunt Hazel does the driving.
I stay in my room, waiting for my father
to explode right there in Uncle Ned's face.
Don't Aunt Hazel and Uncle Ned
know the last thing a person
who drives an ancient brown Studebaker
needs to see when he's short of cash
is someone else's shiny new car?
Aunt Hazel must have been drinking, too,
to let Uncle Ned do such a dumb thing
as come showing off his stupid new car
today, right before Christmas,
when we don't have a spare dime.

Mother starts crying and making apologies
for Uncle Ned
after they leave.
I overhear Daddy let loose with the cuss words
and shout something at her about her
drunken brother and all her
medical bills.
I come out of my room just in time

to see him give a swift kick
to a tire of the old Studebaker
on his way to do some hammering
in the shed.

SATURDAY DOWNS AND UPS

"What's eating you today?"
Beth has such a way of getting
right to the point.

"Well, if you really need to know,
things are just swell at my house."

Uncle Ned's ridiculous visit,
Daddy's blow-up —
I can tell Beth everything
except the details about Mother.
Those details come at too high a price.

"Gee whiz, Laura, I'm real sorry.
I've had a couple of questions I've
been meaning to ask you, but, well,
maybe this isn't the right day."

"Go ahead, try me."
I muster a wicked smile.

"Well, first, have you given art up completely?
I mean, kaput, you know,
forever?"

I'm not ready to tell her all about Mrs. Boucher,
but I get excited going into detail
about my clay family.
I hope describing the pieces I have done so far
will satisfy her.

"So," she says curiously, "I thought the art
contest was just about painting."

"You're exactly right, and these have nothing
to do with the art contest.
I'll let you know when I'm
ready for a private viewing. You'll be the
first to know. Next question?"

"Uh, yeah, Dennis. I couldn't help but
notice your reference to a rodent's rear
when you practically hung up on me the
other day. And, well, it did look
as if Rhonda won the last round
at Megan's party last week.
Have you finally come around to my
way of thinking?"

"Okay, I'm willing to admit
he's a bit full of himself.
I just wish
he'd stop talking to me at all.
That would be easier than this
sometimes stuff, you know what
I mean?"

Beth, who has no more experience dating
than I do, gives me a blank stare.

It occurs to me
that she doesn't know what Dennis is thinking
any more than I do.

Then, since this seems to be
question and answer day,
I blurt out
something I've wondered about
for a long time.

"Beth, you're not jealous, are you?
Of Dennis and me, I mean?
You know, that I . . . that he . . .
that we are, like . . . friends?"

The look on her face is priceless.

But all she'll give me is
vintage Beth.
A deep belly laugh and
"Yabba dabba doo!"
We go back to giving each other a friendly
bad time about dumb things
until we split off at the bridge.
After I'm sure
Beth is well on her way home,
I circle back to town
and head for Simone's.

SATURDAY TEA

Mrs. Boucher is just locking the shop door

when I arrive, but she looks genuinely pleased
to see me.

"Just in time for tea, my dear. It's a Saturday
afternoon ritual, between shop time
and work time."

I suppose by work time she means
working on her own art.
Feeling a lot more relaxed than last time,
I follow her to the back room, where I am
surprised to see my clay family
right where I left it.

She chatters about the exhausting Christmas rush,
how glad she is when it's over.
I join in with positive things,
careful to leave out death
and health issues.
I don't want her to think I'm nothing
but a bag of problems every time I come around.
We banter back and forth as easily as old friends.
She lets the conversation go where it will,
never prying, never nosy
like Aunt Hazel.

She doesn't mention anything about
our first conversation.
She fills me in on herself,
how she studied in Paris at the Sorbonne,
dabbling in all kinds of art —
oil painting, watercolors, pottery —
before settling on sculpture.
She points out some of her favorite pieces

around the shop.

Without asking me if I want to work,
she brings out a fresh supply
of clay and sets it before me
on the workbench.
I spot the wheel
tucked away in a back corner.
"When it's time, Laura,
I'll show you how to throw,
and we'll talk about firing and glazing.
For now, I don't want to interrupt
what you have going here
with the —
with your
clay family.
I think you are on to something
important."

We work silently, side by side.
I lose all track of time
until she says through that
smile of hers,
"I'm afraid, my dear,
that it is time to throw you out."

"I'm just finishing up," I say.
I place the newest creation
with the other figurines
and clean up my workbench.

"Don't be so long
coming back," she says
as I head out the door.

BRAND NEW CAR - FIGURINE #7

A skinny man

leans lopsided

against a fancy new car.

A hefty woman

sits in the driver's seat

both hands on the wheel.

ALL IN THE FAMILY

Rumor has it there might be a raise coming,
maybe first of January.
I can hear the hope in Daddy's voice
through my half-open bedroom door.
He pops another beer.

Mother barely lets him finish before
she jumps in with her own news.
"Paula's going to full time with her new job,
and she's asked me to watch Kim and Jeff.
The little bit she can pay me will help us out,
and she'll still save money on child care."

"Iris, it's too soon. You need to get
back on your feet."

"I'm better, Harold. This new medicine
Dr. Goodman gave me is really making
a difference. He said I needed to get
out of the house. It'll be good for all of
us, you'll see."

An awkward silence,
and Daddy lets it rest.

She did get through
Kennedy's death
and Thanksgiving,
and she does seem better.

Can this be for real?

HELPING HAND

I'm actually looking forward to
the band dinner
now that Mother is acting so regular.
She even offered to help Diane's mom with the food.
I told Diane to tell her mom that my mother
doesn't like to talk about her "blood disease,"
so I hope that stops the questions
about her health.

I volunteered to bring spaghetti.
My sauce has Chef Boyardee
beat by a mile.
Mother dug deep
in the recipe box and
found the one
Grandma used at the hotel.
Daddy took us to Buy-Low
because we didn't have basil,
and Mother helped me
brown the ground round.

I could have done it myself,
but I didn't mind so much,
her working with me.
She talked a bit about
helping in the hotel kitchen
when she was young.

It was peaceful in the kitchen
working side by side.

I kept thinking about the last

youth group meeting,
when Pastor Upton told us
about all those people up in Seattle
getting healed these days.
I need to know what it looks like
and sounds like
and feels like
when someone has been healed.

PRIVATE KEY

The sign on the door at Simone's
says, "Will return at 1:00."
I dig into my purse
for the key Mrs. Boucher gave me last time.
It feels strange, letting myself in.
I try to look like I know what I'm doing,
so someone doesn't think I'm breaking in
and call the police.
I think about how nervous I was
the first couple of visits.
Now here I am
letting myself in with a key
to a place that feels like a second home —
better than a second home,
considering all the
free clay, and quiet,
and Mrs. Boucher's kindness.

The clay family is bathed in the morning sunlight
slanting across the workbench,
but there is something different.

They aren't the way I left them,
I mean, they are the same figurines,
but they are arranged in a circle,
and I definitely left them in a row.
Then I see her note.

"These are so lovely. I hope you'll tell
me the story behind each one someday.
I hope you don't mind if I put them in a circle.
They seem happier that way."

It doesn't take me long to do what I came to do.
It started forming in my head
yesterday
when Mother and I
made the spaghetti sauce.

COOKING LESSON - FIGURINE #8

A smiling woman

and young girl

facing each other

hands immersed

up to the elbows

in a large bowl.

SECOND THOUGHTS

I walk slowly up the dirt road,
now buried under nearly two feet of snow.

I walk slowly so I can replay
the encounter with Mrs. Grant in the hall
today.

"Laura, I would be privileged to take a peek
at your portfolio before you send it off. Be glad
to give any last-minute help."

"Thanks, Mrs. Grant. I'll keep that in mind . . ."

Have I made a terrible mistake?
Could I get back into it, as easily
as my mother has gotten back into life?
Could I throw together a portfolio
before the January deadline after all?
Could I?
Should I?

Dare I
get back to that
get back to that
get back
to
that?

MAKING PEACE

I study our little yellow house
on Seagrove Avenue
with the plastic storm windows
that make even Daddy feel boxed in and anxious
for spring to come sometimes.
Looking out from the inside
can make the cold winter days look gloomier
and grayer than they really are,
especially for someone
like Mother,
who sat in there all by herself all day

until recently.

Now things are different.
Paula picks her up early in the morning
and brings her home late in the afternoon.
All the going and coming
has freshened the stale, smoky, oil-burning air,
blown some new life into our house,
into Mother.

When I come home
she asks how my day went.
It's worth telling her
because she remembers better now.

Evenings lately
she's been crocheting doilies again,
like she used to do.

When I tell her Beth is coming home with me

after school tomorrow, she looks pleased.
"Been a long time," she says, "since
you brought a friend home."

I smile and nod.

We aren't best friends just yet, Mother and I,
but maybe we can at least make peace.

CHRISTMAS EVE

Daddy takes Mother to the five o'clock mass
while I finish cleaning up.
In a little while
family will arrive.
Paula, Frank, and the kids,
Sandra and her family,
Aunt Hazel, Uncle Ned,
and a bunch of Wahlberg cousins
we only see once or twice a year.

Until recently
I half-expected we wouldn't have the usual
family gathering at our house
on Christmas Eve. Some years
Mother's nerves were too bad,
and this year,
what with the breakdown and all,
well, I just didn't expect it.

But here we are.
Mother will make eggnog

that Daddy will spike with Jim Beam,
although I wish he wouldn't this year,
because Uncle Ned can't seem to quit
when he gets going these days,
and it doesn't mix well with Mother's pills.

Before everyone gets here, Mother and Daddy
will have her traditional oyster stew
while I stick to peanut butter and jelly.
Daddy will tell us again
how they had *lutefisk* and *lefse* on the farm
in Bemidji when he was a boy.

When everybody arrives we'll gather in the small
living room, glowing with Christmas lights and candles.
I'll get down on the floor and play with the kids
crowded around the tree.
Each of them will find a present with their name on it,
little junky toys from Woolworth's I wrapped myself.
The adults will get louder and merrier
with each round of Christmas cheer,
and I will take pictures
with my Brownie Starflash camera.

I wonder
if nervous breakdowns
money worries
alcoholic tendencies
or stormy relations
will bleed through the negatives.

But for this moment
Christmas Eve is aglow
as it should be.

CHRISTMAS DAY

I guess I could be really down about Christmas
this year, but maybe this is one of the first times
I've really considered what Mrs. Samuels
said last Sunday,
about the hope that came into the world
through the birth of the Christ child.

Maybe it is okay to have some hope
that Mother can keep herself sane today
and tomorrow
and the next day,
and take her medicine correctly
and not sit and stare or pace
and stay busy and out of the house
and sleep every night
and give her worries a rest.

Maybe then
it will just keep getting better
and better.

And maybe hope is much more valuable
than all the gifts we didn't exchange this year,
and the peace I feel this day
is the best present of all.

HEALING AND PRAYER

Carla helps her father
pass around hot cider at the youth meeting,

and we all get comfortable.
Pastor Upton sinks into his chair
and fiddles with his collar
like it's too tight.

He checks by show of hands
how many of us know anything
about healing or prayer.
My hand stays down
along with most of the others,
but my heart lurches.

If you only knew how desperate I am
to know how this stuff works . . .

Pastor Upton smiles
"Looks like I know where to begin," he says,
looking more relaxed.

He dives right into healing,
listing off just some of the miracles
in the New Testament
like a grocery list,
stopping to elaborate on a few:

> the man with an unclean spirit
> Peter's mother-in-law
> a leper
> a paralytic
> a withered hand
> the Centurion's servant with paralysis
> the bleeding woman
> the blind man
> a demon-possessed man

I soak up the discussion that follows,
already full of questions I'm afraid to ask,
when Pastor Upton says,
"If we are going to talk about healing,
we need to know how to pray."

He reads to us from the Bible,
        how to pray and not lose heart,
        pray without ceasing,
        pray for one another,
        pray to your Father who is in secret,
        and yes, all things that you ask in prayer,
        believing, you shall receive.

One of the boys raises his hand to tell
how praying for his granny's diabetes
brought her blood sugar under control,
he's sure of it.

A girl wants to know
should she pray for healing
between her mama and papa
even though she doesn't believe
they will ever get back together.
That sparks a lively discussion.
Several agree it would be a waste of time
for her to keep praying a prayer
she doesn't believe in.

Pastor Upton says wait a minute,
she should keep praying
but she should be open to whatever God has in mind
because his ways are not always our ways.

That's the clincher.
How do you know
what God has in mind?

My head is swimming
when Pastor Upton says it's time to go.

"Be sure to tell your parents
about the prayer vigil on New Year's Eve.
Hope to see you there,"
he says, ushering us to the door.

Fat chance.

I want to take up the conversation with Daddy,
and ask him what he thinks about healing
and whether some kind of healing
could be going on with Mother,
and what he thinks about prayer,
but when he picks me up
we have our usual
non-conversation.

PRAYER VIGIL

It's about ten degrees below zero outside.
The stars are so clear you can almost reach up and touch them,
and a foot of new snow crunches under our feet.
Shivers run through my bones —
probably not from the cold
but because I can hardly believe that Daddy and I
are on the way to the prayer vigil at the church.

When he said, “Let’s go,” I didn’t question
why a person who has hardly darkened the door to church
all year and dropped his daughter off shamelessly
most Sunday mornings,
why a person like that would want to go to
a prayer vigil. The first thing I thought
was how pleased Pastor Upton
will be when he sees that his invitation to
an absent parent actually paid off.
At least maybe Mrs. Samuels will stop asking
where my father is every Sunday.

White paper bags with sand in the bottom
and a candle lit up inside line the sidewalk
to the church, and it feels more like we
could be going to a festive party up in the Tremont district
than to church, to pray on New Year’s Eve.
I wish Pastor Upton had given us more
hints about how you go about it,
so you know what God has in mind
for you to be praying for.

We settle into a pew about halfway up,
with a good view of the Christmas tree, and I notice
how warm and cozy it feels with the candles
in the windows flickering every time the big red doors open,
and how good the pine boughs smell.
I look around without being too obvious about it,
like people do on Sunday mornings when they want
to see if their neighbors made it after the late night before,
and in the dim light
I am aware of other shadowy figures
sitting helter-skelter in the sanctuary,
but it’s mostly Daddy’s slightly slouched

shoulders and upturned face
I try to study with sideways glances.
I've never done this before,
a prayer vigil,
and I'm almost sure Daddy hasn't either,
and I wonder how he's going about it,
because I can't seem to get
"I Want to Hold Your Hand" out of my head,
and I can see Dennis Martin's face so clearly
and hear him telling me at Megan's party
within earshot of Rhonda
how fabulous I look
in my red plaid skirt and sweater.
I have to look beside me in the pew to make sure
he didn't slip in while I wasn't looking.
I close my eyes and take some deep breaths
to try and get my thoughts under control
or figure out what God wants me to pray about —
and of course, that's when the garbage starts
really cluttering up my brain.
Images of oil paints,
painted ceramics, a wild-eyed mother,
the lobby of the state mental hospital,
police cars, the 11th Street Bridge,
and a funeral procession
swirl in my head and quicken my pulse
like some kind of crazy dream,
and I open my eyes, wondering how
this could be prayer.

The day that I suggested Mother take up
painting again replays in my head
over and over,
making me want to jump up

and run out into the freezing night.
I want to take it back,
reverse the way it made
her break into pieces,
erase the way it caused her
to be so different,
so strange, so unlike
everyone else's mother.

Daddy clears his throat,
and I want to ask him
is he praying or entertaining
runaway thoughts like I am.
I want to turn to him and confess
like Mother does on Saturday nights,
coming out better
than when she went in.
I want to tell him and God, together,
how sorry I am
for not loving my mother
the way I should,
for wanting to get far away
from her and all her
craziness.

I'm about ready to ask God
if Mother's really been healed,
because it looks to me like she has,
but could he be real clear about it
so I can know for sure —
when Daddy, this person
I feel so close to and so far away from
all at the same time,
signals that it is time to go.

I stand up with a jerk,
feeling both reluctant and relieved,
and I wonder as I follow him out into the cold,
if God will forgive me,
even though I don't know
how to ask him
any more than I know how to ask
my own father.

JANUARY 1964

MEETING HALFWAY

Beth and I meet halfway
across the 11th Street Bridge
for a New Year's Day walk.
With the temperature above freezing
for the first time in weeks,
we open our coats
like new leaves unfurling in the spring.

"I made a killing last night, babysitting," she says.

"Your regulars?" I ask.

"Yeah. He was drunk and
I think he slipped me an extra
ten by accident."

We wind around the canal
that circles the high school like a moat,
and I smile at Beth's comical description
of Mr. Beauty College, that's what she calls him,
fumbling in his pocket for his wallet
before passing out on the couch.

I laugh
as I picture my father in the same condition
last week when he spent a little too long
at the VFW celebrating the raise he got.
Everyone was so relieved
and the climate at our house
was so much better
that Mother didn't even make
the usual fuss over

his having one too many drinks.

We climb the front steps to
the high school and sit
looking out over the large school yard.

"Okay Beth, I'm ready," I say.

"Let me guess, Laur. I've got it.
You are finally ready to admit I am
totally right
and you are totally wrong
about Dennis Martin."

"You are one hundred percent wrong,
and lucky I'm in such a good mood,
my friend." I give her a friendly nudge.
"I'm ready for the sneak preview of my
clay figures. Wanna spend the night Friday?"

Beth gives me a surprised look.
"You know I do, but is your mom,
I mean, a while back you said
she couldn't, I mean shouldn't
have visitors, and . . ."

"She's feeling much better,
in fact, I'm serious,
I think she's been healed
of the,
of the blood disease, you know,
and well, you haven't been over
in forever."

"I'm glad your mother is better,
but what do you mean by 'healed'? You're not getting
all weird about religion,
are you, Laura?"

"Let's save religion for another day.
For now, just enjoy the privilege
of the sneak preview, in spite of your
cruel and scathing assessment
of my sometimes friend,
Dennis Martin."

We both laugh
and head back to the bridge,
savoring the bond
that neither of us
could ever explain.

ASSIGNMENT

First day back after Christmas break
it's hard to hear over the
cafeteria buzz.
Aside from *what didja get for Christmas,*
it's *what didja think of Werner's*
assignment to create your family tree?

Beth says, "No big deal. I have
enough family to fill the chart
already."

Diane says, "My grandparents

found our family crest last year
when they went to Scotland."

Megan says, "My mom's good at
this stuff. Shouldn't be a problem."

I say, "My Great Aunt
Hilda has already done my dad's
whole side."

Maybe this is my chance
to fill in the gaps
on Mother's side
of the tree.

OLD IDEA, NEW IDEA

I hear them laughing when I
come in from school.

"And then he crawled under the bed
and I had to get . . ."

"You must be talking about Jeff again,"
I interrupt, dipping into the cookie jar.

"He's a little dickens, he is. Wants to climb
or run everywhere out of reach.
But I can usually bribe him back with a cracker.
We have a good time together, though,
and when Kim comes in from school the time flies.
I'm glad I'm able to help Paula."

I watch Daddy nod and smile from his perch
on the kitchen stool.
Seems like she's convinced him
this is a good idea after all.

If he's convinced,
I'm convinced.
I can't deny how good it feels
to have a mother
driven by something
other than
worry.
"Is it okay if Beth spends the night
on Friday?"

Mother stops slicing the tomatoes to give me
a curious look. "Of course it is,
but I thought you weren't interested
in that anymore, it's been so long."

I look straight at her.
"I never did lose interest
in having friends over.
It just didn't seem like
a good idea for a long time.
You know what I mean, Mother?"

In her eyes
I see a flash of pain
that softens into
acceptance.

She doesn't say anything,
but I think we just connected.

FOUND OUT

"Something's missing," Beth says.
"It's been so long since I was here.
What's different?"

She looks around the room,
puzzled.

I don't help her out.

"Your art stuff, Laura. It's gone.
The easel, the paints. Did your father
finally enforce a clean-up campaign?"

I sink down on the side of the bed,
full of shame,
as if Beth had walked in on Dennis and me
going way too far, as if that would ever happen.
This wasn't a good idea,
bringing Beth home.
My own mother can handle visitors
better than I can.
Anger finally opens my mouth.

"Beth, I brought you home
to see my clay figurines. Can we
leave it at that?"

She settles on the bed next to me
and presses on.

"You didn't enter the art contest after all."

It's a statement, not a question.
Detective Beth has figured it out.
I'll bet she's figured out there is
no blood disease, either.

"But why, Laura? Everyone knows
you're, you would have been, a shoo-in.
Whoa! Does Mrs. Grant know?
She was counting on you to win for us,
for our school,
you know, school pride,
and besides, she really cares about you.
Why, Laura?"

I think about how things are
so much better at home,
and how good I feel about working
with clay and Mrs. Boucher,
and how Beth and I have been
best friends forever

but something
buried so deep I can't get to it,
something keeps me
from saying more than
"I have my reasons, Beth,
but not now. I'm not ready
to talk about them
right now. Do you still
want to see my clay
figurines? You'd better say
yes, because I hauled
them all the way home from
Simone's just for you, my friend."

"Bring 'em on. You know I do!"

And I know
once again
Beth is a true blue
best friend
forever.

ART APPRECIATION

The Gerard kids
take longer
than usual to quiet down.
I sink into the nearest chair,
making a mental note to abandon the tent-fort idea.
It only prolongs the evening.

I survey the mess,
too tired to put any music on,
when I spot a new painting —
a stark new painting,
in a corner across the room.

I can't tell if it's a male or female,
but whatever or whoever it is,
its shape fills a tall, narrow canvas
top to bottom,
and it's draped in a dark, swirling,
cape-like robe.
I move up for a closer look
and really start to get spooked
looking at the chalk-white face,

because it looks out at you
but really past you
with piercing dark eyes
that are tormented, pleading.

I step back and shiver, as if making way
for the creature to pass by
or jump out and grab me,
and I nearly scream in terror
when the door opens
and the Gerards walk in.

"I'll get this mess cleaned up,"
I say, shaking, recklessly
attacking the tent fort.

"What do you think?" Mrs. Gerard says,
watching me curiously.

"I, um, I'm sorry I didn't get this mess . . ."

"I mean the painting. I saw you looking at it. What
do you think?"

I'm not sure what I think.

"It's . . . uh . . . stunning."

She laughs. There is a long, uncomfortable
pause while her eyes pierce right through me.
She offers no elaboration or explanation.
Finally she says, "You seem . . . interested."

Since it wasn't a question,

I don't feel like responding.
I nod and head for the door,
hoping Mr. Gerard and his car keys
are not far behind.

NO FEAR

Beth and I walk to the library on Saturday,
and I do most of the chattering,
filling her in on the growing pottery family
and my arrangement with Mrs. Boucher.
Of course I don't go into detail about all the things
Mrs. Boucher and I have in common,
the crazy stuff,
but Beth says she can tell by the way I talk
that I like the lady.

"She's amazing," I say.
"Maybe you can meet her someday."

Beth says she's seen her around town,
and she doesn't exactly look like she grew up
in Crawford Hills.
"Brilliant observation, my dear Watson.
Maybe that's why I like her," I say.
I switch to Mrs. Gerard's latest
painting.

"If she's trying to copy Edvard Munch's
The Scream, she's doing a pretty good job.
It had me so spooked, and then they walked in,
and I practically jumped out of my skin."

"I told you she's a nutcase," Beth says.
I hardly listen to Beth go on about
Mrs. Gerard. I'm stuck on her last
words to me

you seem interested

you seem interested

you seem interested

Do I?
I wonder.
Am I interested in painting again,
or am I still afraid?

Will something in me get broken
if I take up a brush
again?

I pounce on the sidewalk
like I'm the dot at the bottom
of a question mark.
Beth gives me the
"you're being weird again" look.

No.
I'm not afraid.

I'm on to something way better
than painting.
Something that speaks
to my fingers,
way down to my soul.

No.
I am
not
afraid.

JUST IMAGINE

You can't tell me Mother hasn't been healed.
There is a new look in her eyes,
but not the crazy kind.
She's happier than I've ever seen her.
She sleeps like a log
and enjoys getting out of the house
to take care of the kids.

So maybe Daddy *was* praying on
New Year's Eve after all,
and I know Grandma
prays all the time.
Maybe there were more prayers mixed in with
my wandering thoughts than I realize.
In that case,
I was praying on New Year's Eve, too.

Or maybe it's an outright miracle
like the kind Pastor Upton says is happening
all over the Northwest these days.

I embarrassed myself Sunday in
Mrs. Samuels's class when I blurted out
that I knew someone who has been healed.
As soon as I said it I regretted it,

because everyone wanted to know
who
and what
and how
and, of course, I didn't want to go
into the whole story,
so Mrs. Samuels sort of rescued me,
thanked me for sharing,
and on the way out
she said, "Don't forget to thank God, Laura,
for the healing."

So, thank you, God,
for making my mother normal again.

Just imagine the possibilities
of having a normal mother.

PUZZLING MUSIC

When I try to play
Tchaikovsky's "Dance of the Reed Flutes,"
it sounds more like
circus music
during the clown act,
it's so pitiful.

But Daddy's eyes sparkle when he peeks in my room
to smile his approval
and let me know he's taking Mother
to her ceramics class.

I think it doesn't really matter
how well I play it
but that I try playing it at all.
The sheet music was one of the only store-bought
gifts I got for Christmas,
and I know it makes him happy
to hear me play the flute,
even though I think he knows
by now that I'm not going to be the world's next
great flautist.

I stop playing after I hear them leave, and I
watch the old Studebaker chug down the hill
in the bright moonlight
with the frozen snow glistening all around
like precious jewels.
I catch the silhouette of the two of them
in the front seat.

It occurs to me
that the love they share
is both mysterious and haunting

like the song of the reed flute.

LOPSIDED TREE

My family tree isn't symmetrical
like a perfect Christmas tree.
It's lopsided,
scraggly,
leaning dreadfully to one side

from the prevailing winds
and weather.

On Daddy's side
we have names, dates, and birthplaces
going back practically to the Vikings.

Great-grandparents Gunhild and Rasmus
came by sailing vessel from Stavanger,
traveled overland by wagon,
and took homesteads
in the Red River Valley
near Halstad, Minnesota.

They were a sturdy stock
of hardworking Lutherans —
alive in my mind because of
Daddy's stories.

Nobody seems to know
or want to offer
much of anything
about Mother's side,
least of all Mother.
We sat down together last night,
and she got out the few pictures she has —
my swaggering elusive grandfather,
standing in front of his saloon,
rumored to have the longest mirror in the west,
my prim and proper grandmother
with English roots
on the steps of the big pillared house.

Missing from the pictures were the details,

how he lost his wealth and his mind along the way,
departing this earth after a long, dark decline
leaving nothing but
unanswered questions behind.

I suppose every family tree
has its weaker branches.
I wish mine
didn't look so diseased.

TO THINE OWN SELF BE TRUE

Beth avoids asking me
to go to the National Guard Armory tonight
to hear who won the art contest,
and when Diane brings it up,
Beth shushes her like a parent
scolding a child in church.

I've already decided tomorrow
would be a good day
to be sick.
I'll give it time for the excitement
(disappointment)
to die down.
I'll leave like I'm going to school
and sneak down to Simone's.
Mrs. Boucher and I can
get some real planning done
on my new career as a potter.
Maybe tomorrow would even be a good day
to begin learning about the wheel.

Yeah, that's what I'll do.

Last year wasn't a lost cause, though.
I know what it means now,
to be true to thine own self.

Don't try
to be something
you
are
not.

I am not a painter.

I am a potter.

CLOSURE

The first thing that goes wrong on this wintry day
is Diane's mom honking me over
to the curb and insisting I accept
a ride to school.
My heart sinks so low
it feels ready to drop out of my chest.
I'm hardly settled in the backseat of their
Chevy Bel Air station wagon before hearing
Diane's complete rundown
of the art contest winner,
some wild-lookin' guy from Lake County
whose winning piece,
according to Diane,
might as well have been used

as a paint drop on some construction site.

"I hear you didn't enter this year,"
Diane's mom says, peeking over her shoulder
at me, slumped down in the backseat.

"That's right."

"Well, if you had
you would have beat this guy out,
that's for sure.
It's a shame what passes for art these days."

I start feeling better. Maybe it won't be
such a bad day after all
if everyone agrees with her.

As the day progresses,
a few do, a few don't.
Those in the "don't" category
seem to think I messed up
a chance for Crawford High
to shine in the spotlight.
I hesitate to point out that I also messed up
a chance for a free ride to the Art Institute.
That's assuming I had won,
of course. I'm almost through this horrible day
when Mrs. Grant corners me at my locker.
"Come into the workroom for a minute, Laura,"
she says.

I have no choice.

"I'm sure you've had a day, and I don't want

to add to it. You're still the winner
in my book, and if you ever want to talk
about it, you know where to find me."
She gives me an awkward hug
and then looks intently interested in
finding something in her top drawer.

More relieved than anything else,
I thank her and hurry into Werner's class.
I'm too exhausted to worry about Dennis.
I figure he will continue
ignoring me as well as he has
since the campaign, and then this awful day
will be over.

All eyes are on me as I hurry in late,
and before I slide into my chair
Dennis flashes a smile
that causes my knees to weaken.
After my heart slows down from
a race to a trot, I feel a strange calm.

Dennis passes me a note:
"So, I'm sorry you didn't win,
but guess you can't win
if you don't try. Have you
given up?"

Instead of writing back
I turn fully around and hiss,
"Not on your life, Dennis Martin,
not on your life."

He flashes his gorgeous smile,

and I smile right back
through a deep blush.

For someone who hasn't won a contest,
I feel a triumphant sense of victory.

FEBRUARY 1964

CAUSE FOR CONCERN

Mother sits at the table with coffee and a cigarette,
her usual post in early morning,
not late afternoon.
She's pumping the one crossed leg
like she does when she's nervous,
something I haven't seen in a while.
My heart does a flip-flop,
something *it* hasn't done in a while.

"What's up, Mother? Jeff give
you a bad time today?" I grab some
chips and plop down on the couch.
An uneasy feeling crowds my throat.
I study her.

She goes over the day, all of Jeff's activities,
how he played on the swing set
and in the sandbox with his Tonka trucks.
A pretty usual day full of ups and downs,
his usual energy level.
She had to tell him several times
not to swing too high, to get down
out of the swing because she's afraid
the swing set is going to tip over,
even though Frank says it's anchored down fine.

But there's more.
"Several times today he clutched the back
of his head and said it hurt. He's so clumsy,
stumbling over everything. I hope he
didn't injure himself somehow when I
wasn't watching. I'm with him

every minute. I just don't know . . ."

I want to say it was just a bad day.
Everything is all right.
Nothing to worry about.
It'll be better tomorrow.

Instead, I take up the worry myself
like a hot coal
passing from her hand to mine,
and I can't get Mrs. Boucher's daughter
out of my mind.

BAND AND BAD NEWS

All City Band,
the one the serious musicians drool over.
I could scarcely believe it when
they made the announcement today.
Of course, it means more practice
working on those notes above high C
that come out screeching like
a gaggle of old hens.
Maybe I will need to visit
Mrs. Boucher's less often for a while,
at least until the first concert.

I'm pretty proud of myself and thinking
Daddy will be too, and I've completely
forgotten about Mother's bad day yesterday
when I burst into the kitchen late.
I can tell by the looks on their faces

that something is going on.
I look from one to the other,
dreading the worst.
Still sniffling from an earlier cry,
Mother tells how Jeff came in screaming
from the yard, saying he couldn't see.
She wiped his eyes and looked
for sand and looked for a speck
and looked and looked
and he still couldn't see,
so she called Paula and they rushed
him to the hospital and he's there now
and Paula will call when they know anything.
It's bad.
Mother breaks down into sobs.

I put my hand around her quivering shoulder
as much to calm my own rising hysteria
as hers.

Thoughts jolt my brain like lightning.
Mrs. Boucher's daughter's symptoms,
clumsiness, blindness . . .
Batten disease?

Dear God, anything,
anything but that.

A CLOSED DOOR

Somehow I sleep through it all,
Paula's phone call before dawn

saying emergency surgery removed a tumor
the size of a golf ball from the base of his brain.
They think they got it all and thank God,
it's not malignant.
He will regain his sight, and they will need
to watch for seizures,
but he will be fine.

This I get from Daddy
while he fixes my breakfast.
"And Mother?" I ask, piling a whole bag
of questions into one.

His voice jars me like a heavily slammed door.
She needs to rest, and there will be
no more taking care of Paula's kids.
It's too much for her,
simply too much for her to handle.

But what about her new life, how happy
she's been, how good it is for her to have
something to do, to get out of the house
every day? Why can't she get back
to taking care of Jeff after he gets better?
She can handle that. I know she can.
She's been healed,
hasn't she?

I want to scream out at him,
but on this subject,
the subject of Mother,
we've never been
able to talk much,
only speculate

each on our own,

and on my own
an icy fear returns.

THE SOUND OF BREAKING CHINA

I hear banging and crashing sounds
before I get to the back door.
I think Mother must be trying
to hang a picture,
that's it,
and it must have fallen to the floor and broken.
When I reach for the doorknob
something hits the other side of the door,
and I jump back away from it, scared out of my skin.
I hear her voice.
She's moaning.
My heart feels like it's going to jump out of my chest.
Is someone in there with her?
Is she . . . are they hurting her?
I listen for another voice, but I don't hear anyone else.
I'm about to run for help when the sounds
move to the other end of the house
and then get muffled,
so I take a chance and open the door a crack to peek in.
I see her crawling on the floor in her nightgown,
ripped off one shoulder, and there's blood everywhere.
Her hands and knees are cut and bleeding,
and I don't see anybody else, so I step in and start
to say something when she hears me
and turns toward me. She picks up a bloody piece

of broken china, Grandma's best china,
the hotel china, like she's ready to throw it,
and struggles to her feet,
stepping on her nightgown so it almost comes off.
Her arm is dripping with blood,
her hair tangled, matted with blood.
Should I run for help?
Oh my God, dear God
help me, oh my . . . the phone starts ringing
and I'm unable to move, frozen with fear.
What if she answers it? What if she doesn't?
She picks it up and hurls the whole thing
against the wall, knocking the receiver off
and sending phone parts flying.
I can hear a voice at the other end.
She looks up and sees me,
seems to see me,
starts toward me swearing words,
vile words I never heard her say before.
"Come here!" she screams.
"Come here right now,
before you get hurt,
get out of the way
get out of my way
before you
before I hurt . . ."

She has a pile of plates in her hand,
raised over her head
ready to hurl at me.
I take off running, and I hear the plates shatter
against the door just after I get outside.
If I hurry I can get to Aunt Hazel's in ten minutes.
A wet snow is falling, and it's slippery.

I run as fast as I can until I'm out of breath,
and I keep running, looking back
to see if she's coming after me,
slipping, falling, crying,
screaming, "Help me, somebody please help me."
A horn honks, and I am panting, racing.
I turn to look as Aunt Hazel pulls up
to the curb with a cigarette dangling out of her mouth.
She waves her arms wildly,
motions me in. I'm sobbing hysterically.

Why did Daddy leave her alone?
Why, why? I knew this would happen.
Why, why?
Oh my God, she's going to kill someone;
me, she's going to kill me.
Oh my God.

The ambulance and the police get there as we pull up.
Someone makes me stay in the car,
makes me drink something, holds my hand,
tells me it's going to be all right,
tries to turn my head when

they take her away.

HURTING BAD

Daddy and I don't talk right away,
but that's not unusual.
The drink they gave me made me sleepy,
and I slept through to this morning.

Daddy puts on his stern voice
when I beg to stay home from school
because I really don't feel good at all today
with a throbbing headache and a general
sick-all-over feeling, and that's the truth for once.
He doesn't give in about school,
says it would be the best place for me today,
but when I refuse to go to Aunt Hazel's this time,
he doesn't put up a fuss.
We'll make it okay on our own, he says,
looking every bit like a kicked-down dog.
I'd feel sorry for him
if I weren't so angry.
He's the one who left her alone
when he should have seen this coming.
In fact he did see this coming.
I know he did.
So why didn't he do something to keep this
from happening all over again?

We clean up most of the broken china.
Daddy puts the phone back together and
neither of us says a word.
Aunt Hazel, whose specialty is cleaning,
arrives a few minutes later with buckets, rags,
and cleaning supplies.
She looks around and shakes her head,
says the place looks like a massacre.
Daddy gives her a dirty look,
and I'm waiting for him to let loose with the swearing,
mad as he is,
but she keeps going,
says she'll try and get the blood
out of the carpet and off the walls,

but there isn't much she can do about the chips and
holes in the plaster.
She looks straight at Daddy
and says Grandma would be better off
not knowing about the china.
I really think she's pushed him too far by now,
so I jump in and say,
"Don't you think Grandma needs to know
why her daughter is gone again?"
Aunt Hazel just sighs and says that's up to my father.
My father walks sullenly to the shed
without a word.

Paula won't be making us any meatloaf, either.
She's had to lay off work and says it will be
a full-time job taking care of Jeff.
She says she thinks the breakdown is all her fault,
letting Mother taking care of the kids.

When Beth and Diane ask me
what's wrong at school, I tell them
I have cramps. It's true in a way.

Everything inside and out
hurts bad, so bad
deep down
and so very bad.

HARMLESS DREAM

Paralyzed with fear and heart racing
I sense her hovering over me so close

sucking the air out of me
by her closeness

her face like greasy snow
dripping onto the black robe
leaving red droplets splashing onto me
and watch out she has a weapon

she's suddenly so tall
hovering higher over me
getting ready to strike the blow
it already sounds like broken glass

and everywhere is red broken glass
she stands in the middle of it
washes her face in it before lifting the weapon
and shrieks of laughter come from her

or me

it's a paintbrush
and she
just wants
to
paint
me.

DEAR GOD

I can't pray anymore,
I can barely think anymore

get out of the way
get out of my way

but if I could talk to God, this is
how it would go:

First of all, what happened with the healing?
I thought she was healed.
I was convinced she was healed.
There were so many signs
she was healed.
So what went wrong?
You tricked me into thinking she was healed,
and I am burning up with anger.

get out of the way
get out of my way

Secondly, you know I can't stay here.
She'll be home in a month,
and I need to leave before she gets back.
You know she tried to kill me.

get out of the way
get out of my way

She hates me.
I know because she used all that foul language
and tried to throw that pile of plates at me,
and then she started to come after me.

get out of the way
get out of my way

Third, I don't believe prayer works.
Like I said, I'm just getting this off my chest.
You won't be hearing from me again.

THE SEWING PROJECT

Sometimes school keeps my mind
off of the problems,
and sometimes it makes things worse.
Today, things got worse.

Now dumb, stupid Honeycut
assigned a dumb, stupid sewing project —
a blouse and skirt with a dumb, stupid zipper
to be worked on mostly outside of class.
She didn't bother to say what people
like me are supposed to do,
people who don't have a sewing machine
or a mother standing by
to give any kind of help.
And to top it all off,
we have to model the dumb, stupid outfit
at some kind of dumb, stupid tea
for our mothers in April.

I avoid Beth and Diane after school
because I'm sure to start crying.
I need to walk home alone and think,
try to think, sort things out
and think.
I stop at the canal,
drop my book bag,

and lean over the railing to stare and stare
for a long time.
Just stare into the murky, half-frozen water below.
I get a handful of rocks and throw them in
one at a time,
throw them hard as I can
and follow their smooth descent to the bottom.
I watch a pelican
cruise along the canal,
swoop down for a fish
without much effort at all.

I scream out to the bird,
"Get out of the way,
get out of my way,
before I hurt you."
I pick up a pile of rocks and start hurling them
toward the big bird,
"Get out of my way
you crazy, ugly bird . . .
out of my way, ya hear?"
The pelican drops the fish.
I threw its timing off,
chased away its concentration.
I'm immersed in an odd sense of power
when I realize that someone
is approaching from behind.
I turn around stiffly
and gasp when I'm suddenly
face to face with Dennis.

Get out of the way.
Get out of my way
Dennis Martin

before I hurt you . . .

"Hey, Laura,
what did that poor bird do to make
you so mad? I thought
you had a special place in your heart
for pelicans. I'll bet this has
something to do with art, right?"

"Maybe, maybe not.
I'm just feeling angry.
Angry at the whole world
about things I can't explain,
so I wouldn't hold it against you
if you didn't understand."

I surprise myself and give him a half smile,
and then I turn back toward the canal,
concentrating hard on tracking
the flight of another pelican.

"Wow, Laura. I had no idea. I mean,
whatever it is sounds pretty serious."

He presses in closer to put an arm
around me. I step away and shrug it off.
"Whoa. I don't think Rhonda would like
it if you do that."

For the first time since I've known him,
Dennis looks serious.
He stretches his arm straight out,
palm out like a cop stopping traffic.

"Now it's my turn.
I need to tell you something,
and maybe it won't be so hard to understand.
Rhonda and me, well, we're history."

Is this for real? Is he for real?
Do I believe him
or not?

He has my full attention now.

"And for your information, I went to your locker
looking for you, and Beth told me she thought
you headed this way. I came to tell you
I'm sorry for the way I've treated you.
I do care about you, Laura.
I care a lot, and well, I thought maybe we could
like, reevaluate our relationship."

I burst into giggles
and stop when I see the look
on his face.

"I'm not laughing at you. It's just that you sound
like a teacher, you know, reevaluating
our relationship and all."

"Well?"

I realize he's serious
and waiting for some kind
of answer.

Will you go with me?

Will you be my girl?
Want to go steady?

He leans toward me,
his voice strong and clear.
"Seriously. Can we start over?
Howie's having a little party
Saturday night at his pad on the lake.
A little dancing,
maybe some beer.
What do you say?"

I search his deep blue eyes for
tell-tale signs of sincerity.
There's only one way to find out
if this is for real.
If he is for real.
If we are for real.

"Okay, Dennis, you're on.
Let's start over."

BIG FAVOR

Beth looks a little surprised
and maybe a little hurt
when I catch up with her
by the lockers. I've avoided
everyone
most of the week,
including her.

"You've got circles under your eyes.
Are you okay?" she says.

"Yeah. I'm fine. Just not
sleeping well lately."

"Is your mother sick again?"

Somehow I half-expected her to ask that question,
so I'm sort of prepared to give an answer,
an honest one,
even if it's not the whole honest one.

"You guessed it. Back to the hospital,
and you know that throws everything off.
It's me and my dad again, for a while."

"I'm sorry," Beth says. "Same thing?"

"Yeah. Same thing.
Hey Beth, I have
a favor to ask."

She gives me her full attention
while words come spilling out of my mouth
that take us both by surprise.

Would she mind if I tell my dad
I'm spending the night
at her house on Saturday,
but I'm really going
to a party with Dennis,
maybe overnight?
I take a deep breath in,

while she lets a loud one out.

"Laura, I can't believe this.
Have you finally gone bananas?
You are playing with fire, I don't mind
telling you.
Playing with fire!"

"Beth, it's not what you think, really.
I know you can't see it,
but Dennis
is decent.
I just want to hang out with him,
get to know him,
and with my mother gone,
I just know
my father's not going to let me go.
That's all."

"But are you really going to
spend — the — night — with — him?"

"Of course not! I'll have Dennis bring me
home, and I'll just tell my dad you got sick
or something
and we had to cancel
the overnight."

Won't I?
Isn't that what I'll do?
Just have Dennis bring me home
after the party,
after all that beer?

She sighs. “Dennis 88 Fingers Martin
is just going to drop you off
instead of taking full advantage of you, is that right?
If this backfires,
don’t say I didn’t warn you.”

She stops and stares at me
for a long moment,
like she’s thinking just how
to say what she has to say.

“You know, that question you asked me
a while back, about being jealous?
The answer is . . . well the answer is
a big, fat maybe I am
sometimes.
But right now, Laur,
I am more concerned about you
than jealous.”

Now I stare back at her,
unable to find any words
at all.

“Oh, and by the way,” she says,
“whatever happened to Rhonda?”

I shrug my shoulders,
stretch my hands out palms up,
and look as dumbfounded
as I feel.

SATURDAY NIGHT

I arrange to have Daddy drop me off at Beth's.
I tell Dennis I'm staying with her,
but since it's so hard to find her house,
I'll meet him at the bottom of the hill.
Everything is in place
except me.
I haven't slept, really, for two nights.
Lights are too bright again.
Feels like light creeping into my head
will explode out my eye sockets.
Sounds, voices, her voice
swirl in my head like an echo chamber.

maybe it's because the sun is shining
I could never get back to that
get out of my way
my way
my way

Dennis flashes his famous grin,
and I settle into his dad's
sleek black Buick Riviera hardtop coupe.
I'm reminded I'm in the company
of a rich kid from the Tremont district.
I decide not to hold that against him tonight.

He motions me to move across the big front seat
next to him. I feel as awkward as a duckling,
but I slide over.

"What's going on?" he says, turning his head
to look me squarely in the face.

My heart lurches.
Just great.
He's heard about my crazy mother,
and he's going to ask a bunch of questions,
and when he satisfies his curiosity
that will be the end of . . .
I lurch toward the door and reach for the handle.

"Laura," he says, almost shouting. "For God's
sake, you look like death warmed over, you're angry
at the world, you've all but abandoned
the one thing that makes you happiest,
and you really ought to give up lying,
because you don't do it very well."

See, I knew it. He knows everything.
Now she has ruined this part of
my life, too.

"What exactly are you talking about, Dennis Martin?"

He starts the engine, and I think
fine, take me home,
but instead of home,
or Howard's party,
he drives up to "C" hill,
with the big white C for Crawford High
the seniors paint on rocks every spring,
where everyone goes to make out,
and I think I should be scared to death,
but really I'm shivering
in excited anticipation.
At the top of the hill
he kills the motor

and takes up the conversation
almost mid-sentence.

"Look, I've kept plenty of secrets myself
and I'm not asking for details,
but let's talk, Laura, I mean really talk.
We were supposed to start over
tonight, remember? I'm ready to listen.
So start talking."

First, I start breathing again,
then I stare at him in utter admiration,
then I cry
and talk
and cry.

RECAP

"So?" Beth says Sunday afternoon
on the phone.

"So thanks a million for covering for me
with my dad and all," I say.

"Sure thing, but what about . . . ?"

I know
exactly what she wants,
but I can't bring myself to tell her
that Dennis Martin now knows
more about my darkest secrets
than she does,

right down to
what I plan to do
before
my
mother
returns.

"Did you . . . ?"

"No, I didn't. For your information,
we spent the evening on "C" hill
talking
talking
talking
not
necking
necking
necking.
He took me home
and yes,
he kissed me
goodnight."

Stunned silence.
For once,
Beth has nothing
to say.

MARCH 1964

BLOW UP

Beth says she's worried about me.
Am I losing weight on purpose?
Circles under my eyes,
jumpy.
"What's wrong with you, anyway?
Why are you so touchy?"
she says, wolfing down her lunch
while I pick at mine.

"What are you, my keeper?
Just leave me alone."
I grab my tray and stand up
so fast I feel light-headed.

They all stare at me,
Diane, Megan, and Beth,
whispering,
watching
as I practically trip over the bench
on my way to the trash
to dump my tray,
running out of the cafeteria,
crying.

I head for the nurse to tell her I'm sick,
really sick,
and I need to go home.
I convince her without having to mention
any of the crazy voices in my head
that haunt me.
Now along with Mother's voice
it's Dennis's . . .

go after it, Laura
ask questions
dig for answers
don't run
dig

WORKING THE CLAY

I leave school and break into a run,
suddenly desperate
to see Mrs. Boucher,
the back room,
my clay family.

I burst through the door so frantically
that she rushes around the counter,
looking over my shoulder to see who
might be chasing me.

"What is it, Laura dear?
What on earth?"

So much has happened since I saw
her last. I start babbling
out of control,
out of breath.
Jeff, the tumor,
the nightmare day, the hospital,
the sewing project,
the voices in my head,
and Dennis, and . . .
Without a word she flips the door sign over

to read “Be back in an hour”
and gently leads me to the back room
like she’s leading a blind person.
She sits me down, brings a glass of water,
and waits while I calm down.
I tell her I have a plan
before my mother returns,
but I probably don’t have much time
before I come down with whatever she has —
maybe I need to quit the clay
before it gets to me, too.

When I run out of words, she says,
“Now then, now that you’re back,
we can both get back to our work, can’t we?”

I look at her in horror.

Did she hear what I said
or is she playing some kind of game with me?
What is she, another crazy lunatic?
Am I starting to attract crazy people
like spoiled meat attracts flies?

I jump up and start to leave,
but she gently catches my hand.
“Sit down, my dear. I know that’s not
what you expected me to say.”

She takes over the conversation,
demanding my attention.
“My daughter’s name was Jeanette.”

Mrs. Boucher describes her daughter’s last years,

how her vision went
before her mind totally lost touch with reality.
Clay became her lifeline,
her only reality.
She and her daughter worked together at first,
making simple shapes.

"Toward the end, she wasn't able to do much more
than hold the cool, damp clay in her hands.
It always brought a smile to her face."

Mrs. Boucher looks straight at me and smiles.

"She kept working the clay, Laura.
Right up to the end, as much as she gave to it,
it gave back to her."

"Well, maybe I'll stay and work for a while,
considering I left school early. But this
might be the last time."

Mrs. Boucher hands me a large clump
of cool clay
while Dennis's voice plays in my head —

dig for answers, Laura
don't run,
dig

DIGGING - FIGURINE #9

Young girl

grasping shovel handle

body bent at waist

eyes focused on ground

right foot poised to dig.

APOLOGY ACCEPTED

I apologize to Beth
before first period. She goes out of her way
to be nice, extra nice.
Maybe she's afraid
I'll break into a million pieces
like one of my clay figurines shattering
onto a hard surface.

"Listen,
my mom says to tell you
she and her sewing machine are on loan
if you need help with Honeycut's project.
Wanna come over after school today?"

I do.
I search Beth's face and words
to make sure my best friend and I
are back in business as usual.
We are.

Their run-down house smells like Mrs. Watson's
famous orange rolls when we come in.
Beth's youngest brother and sister are pushing each other
away from the TV set, because one wants
to watch Rusty the Clown and the other
wants Flintstones reruns.
In the same breath,
Mrs. Watson calmly orders them to settle it
or turn it off while she tells me to put my blue poplin down
and help myself to one of the rolls.

Beth's sister

hangs around with sticky fingers,
asking questions like
"Are you moving in with us?"
That cracks me up,
and I laugh hard for the first time
since *that day*
and get a warm-all-over,
cozy feeling like you get under the hair dryer
at the beauty parlor.
After five tries and Mrs. Watson's patient help,
I finally get the zipper in.
I put on the ensemble —
Honeycut's term.
Mrs. Watson tugs at the skirt hem like she means business,

and with pins clenched between her teeth
she tells me to stand up tall.
"You look like a million,"
she says with a big smile on her face.
I return the smile
and stare too long
at her glowing pink cheeks
and twinkling eyes.

She was a nurse before she had all these kids.
She might be able to help.
Dig, Laura, dig.
Ask her questions.
Go ahead.
This is your chance.
Dig.
Never mind she's your best friend's mother.
Dig.

I open my mouth and stumble over the words.
"Thank you for your help, Mrs. Watson."

I take my time walking home
with one completed project in the bag
and one incomplete project
buried deeper
than I am able to dig.

SIXTEENTH BIRTHDAY

It's my sixteenth birthday.
Daddy, Paula, and Grandma
all try real hard to be my missing parent.

Grandma makes a cake.
Paula takes me shopping
for some new gabardine capri pants
and a pair of madras culottes just like Diane's.
Daddy gets me the red transistor radio
with the leather carrying case I've been wanting.

When Grandma asks, "How is Iris doing?"
Paula says she sent a sweatshirt to me
for my birthday
and quickly changes the subject.
Mama did send a sweatshirt,
but I don't ask how she got it,
since they don't let her out.

I guess you could say part of my birthday present
is that Daddy and I are talking again,

as much as we ever talk.

He let on how he feels
like he usually does,
with few words.
Said what I already knew,
that he didn't think she was up
to watching the kids in the first place.

"Then why didn't you stop her?" I ask,
still feeling angry.

"Guess we all like to have hope
once in a while," he mutters,
and he gets sort of a sheepish grin on his face,
like he's embarrassed,
but I know it's the truth,
and I appreciate his honesty.
I nod in agreement,
watching tears form in the corners
of his crinkly eyes.

I can't stay mad at him any longer.
His love for her is real.
He might well be mad at me
if he could get inside my head.

NERVOUS RASHES

Beth taps me on the shoulder
from her seat behind me
in English class.

"Did you know you have a rash
on the back of your neck
and around your right ear?"

I ignore her,
pretend I don't feel her tap
or hear her whisper

because if I respond
I will blow up again
right in the middle
of this class.

Of course I know I have
a rash on the back of my neck
and around my right ear,
just like my mother's
stupid rash.

DOING JUST FINE

Diane's mom calls and asks to speak to Mother.

"Oh, didn't Diane tell you?
She's over in Medford
with my sister.
You know about my nephew, Jeff,
don't you? He had a brain tumor,
but he's going to be fine.
His doctor is in Medford, so they go over
there a lot these days.
My mother goes along to help."

"Well, I'm sorry about your nephew,
but I'm glad he's doing alright.
It's about the PTA annual fundraiser.
Tell your mother I'll
call her next week. I hope you
and your father are doing okay
without her."

I tell her we're doing fine, just fine.

I wonder if part of doing okay
without a mother
is knowing how to lie.

FEAR OF BREAKING

Truth is,
life is far from fine.
At night
lately,
long after Sputnik
wobbles across the sky,
I get nervous,
start counting
shooting stars,
but that doesn't work,
neither does counting sheep
or blessings.

How will I get through
school without
sleep?

Look what sleeplessness
did to my mother.
What if my grades
start slipping?

What

          if

                    I

          start

slipping

          down

                    until

          I

break?

NIGHT TERROR - FIGURINE #10

Girl in bed

lying on back

under heavy mound of covers

eyes enlarged

looking straight out

terrified

hands over ears

mouth wide open

screaming.

RIDE HOME

Dennis catches me
off guard after Werner's class.
"Laura, wait up
and I'll give you a ride home."

My heart leaps,
and I smile when I think how different
things are since our "hot date."
Sure his attention gets me going,
but ever since that night
when I told him more about myself
than my best girlfriends know,

we've become real friends.

After I finally stopped sobbing and blubbering
that night, he opened his soul to me,
how his hard-driving dad has Dennis's future
seamlessly mapped out for him —
getting into Gonzaga like his older brother,
being a big splash on campus,
taking over the family business,
even the type of girl he should marry
and the ideal time to consider it.

It makes sense now,
the way this year has gone.
Dennis makes sense.
The tension is gone.

He meets me at my locker,

leaving Beth and Diane standing
with their mouths wide open.
I shrug my shoulders in mock cluelessness
and follow Dennis,
his words from our last conversation
running through my head.

go after it, Laura
ask questions
dig for answers
don't run
dig

"Laura, you look, um,
like, not so good again.
How are things?"

"You always catch me on the tail
of a sleepless night, that's all."

"Okay. But I want to know what
you've done in the research department.
Your mom's about due home, isn't she?
Did you take my advice?
Did you go digging for answers?
Did you demand
the facts from someone,
anyone?"

I know now he's really trying to help,
so I remind myself to be patient.

"You just don't understand
about our family.

No one talks about anything important,
least of all to me.
I need to handle it
my way now."

"Well, you know I can relate
to the no-talking mode.
The only time my parents talk
is when one asks the other one
to pour a drink."

He hugs me tightly
and kisses me gently
on the forehead.

"Be careful, Laura.
Be careful."

APRIL 1964

RETURN

She's home.

I don't want to talk to her.
I don't want to look at her.
I don't want to think about her.
I don't want to let her near me.
I don't want to be here.

THE MEADOWLARK AND ME

I wake up feeling cold
in spite of the bright April sun pouring into my room.
I sit up in bed and listen
because I hear a familiar sound outside
on the telephone wire.
It's the meadowlark.
I remember when Daddy first told me to
watch for it every year.
He said it's a sure sign
that spring is not far off.
Most years
it makes me feel happy inside,
and I usually stop and try to imitate its
funny, warbled up-and-down song.
Not today, though.

I get dressed quickly and then start
loading the book bag.
Flute —
no, maybe not the flute —

transistor radio,
toothbrush, comb, a few changes of underwear,
an extra pair of pedal pushers and a sweater,
my last seven dollars in babysitting money.
I check to see if it looks enough like I'm going off for
a day of studying.

The blue floral print skirt and matching blouse,
Honeycut's famous "ensemble,"
hangs all freshly pressed and waiting for the big
stupid Fashion Tea on Monday.
The gala event, as she calls it,
with all the proud mothers waiting in the audience
to see their outfits —
the ones they created together with their daughters —
sashay across the stage.

I picture waiting in the wings
trying to contain
the raging panic
when I am convinced
the entire world is aware
my crazy mother doesn't sew
on a machine we don't own
with a daughter
she hardly knows.
I push it out of my mind
because it no longer matters.

I will be gone.

They sit at the table in their usual places
with the usual coffee and cigarettes and newspaper,
as if nothing in their lives, in this house,

had ever gone wrong.
I avoid their eyes
and shove down words
too late to speak.

I grab a banana and tell them
I'm working on a term paper
and I'm headed for the library.

My heart thumps wildly as I head
out the door,
down the hill,
amazed at how easy it was,
terrified at how hard it will be.

No one else is out this Saturday morning
but the meadowlark and me.

HOW LONG

I stop at Applegate Elementary playground
to catch my breath,
more winded from anxiety
than the downhill walk.

Aunt Hazel and Uncle Ned
are probably still in bed,
but the conversation we need to have
requires cold soberness,
and delaying much into the morning
eliminates that possibility.

I rehearse how it might go,
what I need to tell Uncle Ned about my own
struggles to think straight,
night terrors,
sleeplessness,
weird, disconnected feelings,
nervousness that leads to pacing,
yes, pacing,

and I am reminded
this is a portrait of myself
not *her*.

Crazy thoughts.
The thoughts that always
come over me when I'm near the 11th Street Bridge,
like the murky green water is egging me on,
"Come on in, come on down, it will be easy, just do it."
I want these thoughts fresh in my mind
when I lay it all out to Uncle Ned.
I want him to know how close I feel
to losing my own sanity, flipping out
completely and exactly
like my mother.
He needs to know
the questions that float around in my mind
like pieces of a shipwreck in an iceberg sea.
Questions that keep me awake at night.

What is the darkness that followed my
grandfather to his death? Is it the same
darkness that drives my mother to madness?
How long will it be before it catches up
with me?

I see by the sun that it is already mid-morning,
and I get going in a hurry,
because I just don't know
how long it will be.

SHOWDOWN

Aunt Hazel comes to the door in her tattered housecoat,
with hair hanging out of curlers.
I hear Uncle Ned's gravelly voice
calling from the bedroom,
asking with swear words
who the early-morning caller might be.

For the second time today I feel winded,
breathless,
and I can't stop shaking.

"I need to talk to Uncle Ned."

Aunt Hazel looks at me curiously,
as if she knows what's coming,
but she simply sighs,
motions me in, and says, "Just a minute."
Uncle Ned comes shuffling in,
carrying the fumes from last night's drinking with him.
"What's going on?
You come barging in here this early,
like to scare us to death."

Suddenly my tongue and the tears unleash like a floodgate,
and the two of them sit by speechless

as I cry and babble uncontrollably.
In sobbing gasps, I tell them
how it won't go away now,
the fear that whatever has driven my mother crazy
is going to do the same thing to me,
like some kind of thief robbing our family
of sanity, picking us off, one by one.
How it follows me night and day,
so I can't sleep
or even think straight anymore.

"Uncle Ned, you're her brother
and I know you know what it is.
You must tell me.
You MUST tell me what it is!" I demand.
"Am I doomed to get it, too?"

After what seems like an eternity of pleading,
Uncle Ned speaks in a calm, sober voice.
"You aren't going to get it, Laura.
Believe me, you aren't going to get it.
Go on now.
Go on about your life."

I lurch forward in my chair
and glare at him in disgust.

He didn't really just say that.

Calm, cool, collected,
and sober.

How can he sit there and say that to me?

"I don't believe it, Uncle Ned.
You have the truth.
You could tell me the simple truth,
and you just sit there
and
tell me nothing."

He jumps out of his chair
and moves toward me.
About to throw me out,
I think.

But I'm already gone.

BREAKFAST WITH SANDRA

My body aches.
I'm exhausted from all the crying.
My feet and my heart feel heavy as lead.
I leave Uncle Ned's
with a throbbing head and no plan for the rest of the day.
I walk along the canal.
A strong, fishy smell lures the pelicans
into a swooping, diving frenzy.
I pause and listen to the gulls squeal,
and it reminds me of how Sandra sounds
when she gets revved up about something.
For once,
I don't hear the voice
calling me over the edge and down.
I realize I'm not far
from the tiny apartment

where Sandra lives,
and I head in that direction.

She signals me to be quiet as she lets
me into the messy living room.
"Mom's asleep. What are you doing here?"
she whispers, pulling me into the cluttered kitchen
and closing the door.

She fixes breakfast while I talk.
I'm sure my aunt told her all about
Mother's recent breakdown,
but she hasn't heard it from me.
I tell her about the china day,
and how Aunt Hazel picked me up,
and how I thought Mother was going to kill me.
I describe the last month,
the loneliness with silent Daddy.
I tell her about my anger toward him
for leaving her alone when he shouldn't have.
Then I describe the fear that has been growing
inside me like a cancer,
the fear that I am doomed
and that it is just a matter of time
before I get the disease that Mother has,
whatever that disease is.

"At first, you know, I thought
I caused it, at least the one last year.
I got her to start painting again,
and I thought it was my suggestion
that threw her over the edge.
But now I don't know.
Daddy seems to think taking care of the kids

was probably too much for her.
I feel so confused.
My family tree project started me thinking
in a different direction.
Maybe there's something in the family,
you know, a weak link
being passed down.
There is our mysterious grandfather.
Do you know anything about him?"

Sandra shakes her head.
"I know what you know.
That he sat in a chair
staring, not speaking,
just waiting
for a long and slow death."

"But Uncle Ned knows, Sandra.
I'm convinced Uncle Ned knows.
He has to know,
and he won't tell me.
Now I hate him
almost as much as I hate her.
HE KNOWS,
AND HE WON'T TELL ME!"

I am just about to get
to my anger at God
when Sandra says, "I will bless the Lord
at all times; his praise shall
continually be in my mouth."

Her words fall on my frozen heart
with a thud, and I realize our conversation

is over.
I thank Sandra for the breakfast
and leave.

WANDERING

I spend the rest of the day
wandering aimlessly around town —
much, I note, like my mother
once did.

Do I know where I'm going
any more than she did that day?

I avoid the bridge
and the library
and Mrs. Boucher's shop.
At dusk I wander over to Crawford Lutheran.
I hear the organist practicing the hymns for tomorrow.
I shudder to think what kind of trouble she'd cause
if she knew what I was up to, but I take a chance
and quietly slip inside unnoticed.

I spend the night sleeping fitfully in the back of the sanctuary,
glad the heat is cranked for church.
Spring isn't quite here yet, and I just have
one extra sweater.

A slammed car door jolts me awake
in the morning, and I remember it is Sunday.
I barely have time to scramble back out the basement window
before someone enters the sanctuary.

I walk over to the high school
and sit on the steps
out of the way of traffic,
warming myself in the bright morning sun.
I wonder if a police car is out looking for me yet,
like they did the day Mother disappeared.
It doesn't concern me that much
whether they are or not.
My head and my stomach feel equally empty,
and I realize I am hungry for food and
someone to talk to.
Sometime past noon
my feet point toward the back room
where Mrs. Boucher said she sculpts
most Sundays after church.

WORKING SESSION

I'm relieved to see her car parked
by the back door.
I slow down, take some deep breaths,
determined not to frighten her with an entrance
like last time.

"Why Laura, dear,
what a pleasant surprise."
She pushes her stool
away from a half-chiseled piece of marble,
hugs me, looks me straight in the eye.

"Business or pleasure today?"

"Do you have anything to eat?
I'm really hungry."
I'm sure she can see the anxiety in my eyes
or hear it in my voice,
but she doesn't let on.
Without a word, she goes to the small refrigerator
she keeps for her lunch.

"Ah, you're in luck. I was so slammed
yesterday, lunch went by the wayside."

She sets the wrapped sandwich in front of me
and returns to her bench and chisel.
When she doesn't pick up the conversation,
I get a clump of clay and sit at my work table.

"Mind if I work alongside you today?"

She stays focused on her work
but murmurs, "How lovely,"
and I know she means it.

The anxiety begins finding its way
out through my working fingers,
and I start talking.

"I hate her, you know.
She came home, so I left.
I can't be there anymore.
I can't sleep,
I cry all the time,
wondering how long it will be
before I go insane.
I have a rash now, just like she does.

My best friend thinks I'm really going nuts.
I'm mad at God,
and my cousin for pushing God on me,
and my uncle, who knows what's wrong with Mother
but insists on keeping it a secret,
and my father
because,
well, because he just seems to stand by and let it all happen."

I start laughing,
not at what I've said,
well yeah, maybe at what I've said,
because I'm just rambling like a crazy person,
but what's really funny is the absurd
little creature I've shaped
with oversized ears
and a silly grin.

Mrs. Boucher looks up and laughs, too.
"Laura, it looks like you've created someone who is all ears.
Just what the doctor ordered."

I look straight at her.
"You're going to call my parents, aren't you?"

"Nope," she says.
I watch,
puzzled,
as she bustles around,
gets a blanket and pillow from a closet,
and sets them out on the old sofa she keeps
in the back corner,
starts cleaning up her work area,
adjusts the thermostat,

grabs her jacket,
and comes to me, taking my hand.

"You stay here tonight, Laura.
It's safe and it's warm.
Think about the clay.
Your clay family
and your real family.
What you can control
and what you can't.
The power of love and of hate.
You are no nearer insanity than I am.
Use your own good judgment,
and you will make the right choices
come tomorrow.
Think hard
about your work,
what you have done
and what you have left to do.
Good night, my dear."

She's gone, just like that,
and I sit for a long while in the dimming light,
thinking about the conversation we didn't really have
but all that was said.

I feel safe.

Before falling asleep,
I turn out the lights,
close my eyes,
and look at my clay family
through my fingers.

It occurs to me that one is missing,
and I know what I must do
in the morning.

SURVIVORS

The first thing I realize when the sun wakes me up
is that I've just had the best night's sleep
in weeks.

The next realization, besides hunger,
is that this is Fashion Tea day.
I play a few scenarios in my head.
        Being there with Mother,
        being there without Mother,
        Mother being there without me (impossible),
and I quickly push the thoughts out of my head
because I have work to do.

I get a ball of clay out
and surprise myself by how quickly
a satisfying piece emerges,
a young mother with young girl on one hand
and a smaller boy on the other.
I set the figurines to dry next to the rest of the family.

I write a quick note to Mrs. Boucher,
inviting her to check out my newest addition,
thanking her "for everything,"
including the slightly stale banana bread
I found in the back of the refrigerator.

On this morning there is no wandering.
I know exactly where I'm going.

I reach Paula's doorstep
just minutes after she returns
from taking Kim to school
and Jeff to a morning of rehab.

Shock and then rage sweep across Paula's face.
"What, is it your turn now?"
Maybe she thought I was dead by now, I don't know,
and her cheeks turn pink almost immediately
like they do when she's plenty angry.
She steps aside and lets me in.
"Sit down while I call them
and tell them you're alive."
She sighs heavily.
I can tell she's disgusted with me,
and maybe a little relieved.

When she returns from the phone call
she lights into me about the hell
I have put them all through.
How could I be so selfish to do something like this,
run away and worry a mother who can't handle
any kind of worry?
How dare I do this to her, to them?
I let her go on, because I know what she's saying
is true, and I can't deny it,
but I don't feel like apologizing either.

Then, almost like a faucet switching from one
temperature to the other,
her voice tone changes,

and for the first time ever
she starts to talk to me,
really talk to me,
about her feelings, not just the tired feeling
but the deep down feelings,
as if somehow my three-day journey
had shortened the age gap between us.

She tells me about her years of heartache,
her own anger about Mother's illness,
how it affected her growing up,
drove her out of the house to marry so young
and now, the complications of Jeff's tumor.

"I can't change the way you feel, Laura.
Neither can I change the way things have gone with her
and with us. But I do know this. She's still our mother,
and we all have a lot of life yet to live."

I brace myself for a long preachy sermon
on my recent behavior.
Maybe that's what she was planning to do,
but she studies me for a long while
and takes a deep breath,
like she's turning a corner,
taking a different path, unsure what that new path will bring.

"There is something, Laura,

something you need to know,
and I think maybe the time has come.
Yes, maybe you are old enough to know it now.
Our mother
was raped

when she was about your age.
It was a travelling salesman staying at the hotel.
She was plenty smart, you know, gifted, really,
you can tell from her oil paintings.
She and our grandfather had a falling-out,
who knows why,
no one seems to know,
and Grandma sent her to Portland
to get her away from him,
to try her hand at nursing school.
She had the first breakdown
before she even started classes.
They found her wandering around the streets
of Portland, half-naked, incoherent.
After a long hospitalization
she recovered enough to go home,
but she was never the same.
She has struggled with this
all her adult life, in and out of hospitals,
on and off medications.
I've learned to hate that intruder, Laura,
not our mother.
She's just the victim."

I'm stunned
angry
relieved
confused
full of questions.

"But Paula, not everyone
who has something bad happen to them
goes crazy. How do you explain that?"

"I can't. Weak constitution,
poor health habits, who knows?"

"Genetics?"

"You're the straight-A student.
You tell me," she says, almost sarcastically.

I drop it for now
and change the subject.
"How does anybody get to be
who they really are, anyway?"
The question dissolves between us,
its importance evaporates.
We stare across at each other
peacefully
while the air between us
grows clearer and clearer,
and a new bond,
a new sense of unity emerges,
forged out of a mutual realization
that we are a sisterhood
of survivors.

PEACE IN THE MORNING

I spend the night at Paula's, and when I get up
Daddy's sitting in her kitchen playing with Jeff.
Peace fills the air
like a bouquet of spring flowers.
Paula and Daddy
are sharing a pot of coffee.

I sink into his open arms,
smell his tobacco,
feel his morning whiskers.

“I’m sorry.”

“I’m sorry, too.”

Few words, just like before,
but words that count.
I tell him how afraid I’ve been
of her
of my own shadow
of the past
of the future
of the things I don’t understand.
I tell him how hateful I’ve felt
toward her.

He says, “I know, I know,”
and, “It’s going to be okay.”

I want to believe it.
I want to believe it will be okay.

He gets up to leave.
He says my mother is waiting to see me.

I tell him I would like to make
one more stop
before coming home.

DOCTOR'S ORDERS

Daddy parks the car and says
he'll wait, but looking at the parking lot,
it'll probably be a while
without an appointment.

I thank him and walk boldly
up to the receptionist.

"I'd like to see Dr. Goodman, please."

The nurse looks around to see if my mother
is with me, clears her throat, and says
he'll have to work me in, since I don't have an appointment.
In less than twenty minutes
he calls me into his office and greets me heartily
with his firm handshake, big smile, and
"What can I do for you today?"
as if I were shopping for clothes.

I try to push the words out without stammering.
"You offered to help me once, the day I fainted."

He looks confused for a moment,
then as if a light goes on,
he asks me how much money I think we need.

I'm embarrassed, but I keep going.
"Oh no. I didn't come to ask for money.
I came to ask for the whole truth about
my mother. My sister just told me about the rape.
I want to know what it's going to take to drive
me crazy, too."

There.
I sink back in the chair, as if I had just hurled
a heavy object, like a shot put, and am settling in to watch
where it lands.

Dr. Goodman's smile dims, but doesn't disappear.
He just looks at me for a long moment
like he's thinking carefully about
how to answer me.
Then he says he cannot tell me
what the diagnosis is
and that it would serve no useful purpose anyway.
He says that her problems began long ago,
but there is new medicine coming out every day,
and in fact, he believes the one she is on now
is going to turn the tide.

I stare at him coldly, unconvinced.
"How do you know this pill will be any better
than the dozens of others she has tried?"

"There have been major breakthroughs in the use
of psychotropic drugs in the last few years."
He looks carefully at me as he speaks.
"These new drugs are much more effective,
and research is moving quickly and positively
toward better medication for patients
with mental illness
like your mother."

Mental illness.
Mental illness.

The words jolt me,

and for the first time I realize
no one in our family
ever uses the term
mental illness.

"But suppose I get raped, too, or have
some other huge, tragic event in my life?
What's to keep me from breaking down just like her?"

I'm shaking now, close to tears.

He leans toward me and looks directly into my eyes.
"Young lady, I brought you into this world,
and I can tell you,
you are a unique creature
in your own right,
just as your mother was."

"How can you say that, Dr. Goodman? Don't they teach
you anything about genetics in med school?"

I sink into the chair and start sobbing uncontrollably,
hardly caring how rude
my words must sound.
He hands a box of tissues across the desk
and waits patiently for the sobs to subside.
His smile returns.
"Yes they do, Laura, and I'm glad you
brought that up. It sounds like you know,
then, that because you have a
strong, healthy father,
you have a good fighting chance
against this disease."

"But no guarantees, right?"

He shakes his head and sighs.
"Ah, how many times
over these many years
have I been asked that question?"
His eyes narrow and he turns toward the window.
For a long moment
it feels like he floated far away,
lost in search
of the one right answer.
He turns his sad and tired eyes
back toward me.

"There are no guarantees, Laura.
But I can tell you this.
You've seen a lot,
for your young years.
Make it work for you going forward.
Keep asking questions,
demanding answers
and calling the beast by its name.
Life is too short to spend on the pursuit of a guarantee."

I let his words settle over me
like a gentle mist.
I feel calm now
and ready to go home.

I thank him,
even give him a hug,
and walk slowly out to the car.
The image of a shot put
comes to mind again,

and I realize the weight
is out of my hands.
I have no control over it now,
and the farther away it lands
the better.

HOME

"Did you find
what you were looking for?"
Daddy says when I get in the car.

I pause to make sure
the tears will not return
if I speak.

"Daddy, do you think I have
a fighting chance?"

"What do you mean, honey?"

"At being normal,
not like, I mean,
without any
mental illness."
I watch to see if he flinches
at the mention of the beast.

"My dear Laura,
you have better than
a fighting chance in life."

I let out a long, slow breath.

no guarantees
no guarantees

"Thanks, Daddy. I think I
found what I was looking for.
Let's go home."

Mother sits at the table
smoking a cigarette,
the one restless foot swinging
back and forth,
until she sees me walk in.

We hug for a long time without words,
and then she sets about
fixing lunch, as if it were
Saturday, and we had just
come in from shopping.

The phone rings.
"Hey, you big dumb nut.
I called last night and your dad
said you were okay. I just wanted
to hear for myself. Listen, I've
changed my mind about our friend Dennis
Martin. You should have heard
him stick up for you when
Jerry Pruner said you'd finally
gone nuts. Oh, and the biggest
news of all: one of your paintings
is on the cover of the yearbook!
You'll never guess which one."

I'm too tired to talk, but I tell Beth
I have lots to share
when I see her.

It feels strange for me and my parents
to be home on a Tuesday morning
and even stranger knowing
that from this day forward,
home and I
will never be the same.
We'll be better than the same.

FIGURINES AND FORGIVENESS

The discussion doesn't happen right away.
After I am home about a week,
and things are pretty much back
to normal,
yes, normal,
I catch her one afternoon
sitting in her rocker
reading.

"Put your book down, Mother,
please, I want to talk to you."

"What is it, honey? Is something wrong?"

"No, nothing is wrong.
In fact, everything is right.
I mean, everything is really right."

I go into my room and bring out the clay family.
They are lined up in a long, narrow box,
labeled with titles. I pull out "Cooking Lesson"
and hand it to her.

"This is my favorite. It's for you."

I've never seen her face light up
as brightly as it did today.

"These are unbelievable, Laura.
When did you do all this?"

"Over the school year," I say.
I decide to save the details
about Mrs. Boucher and the back room
for another day.

I sit down next to her
and tell her as much as I can
without getting garbled.
How I haven't loved her like I should
because I didn't understand what was going on
and maybe still don't fully understand.
How I need to ask forgiveness
and want things to be different,
in fact, has she noticed
things are different?

In her typical way,
she brushes it off,
says I don't have need for forgiveness,
but of course she forgives me,
and she understands my confusion and frustration,

and she doesn't hold anything against me,
and she loves me very much.

I'm not sure if she gets it at all,
what I am trying to say,
but the important thing is
I get it,
and I did what
I needed to do,
and it feels as good
as anything I have ever done.

I wouldn't want to say it,
but I think there has been some healing
in our family
after all.

AFTERWORD

Crazy is loosely based on events and experiences from my own life. Because loved ones have been diagnosed with bipolar disorder, and misdiagnosed with schizophrenia, I have a great appreciation for proper diagnosis and treatment of mental illness. I have seen firsthand the positive effect that a strong support system can have on the person experiencing the illness as well as other family members. As in Laura's case, that support may be found outside the home, at school or at church, and in unlikely places, such as back-room art studios.

Bipolar disorder, sometimes called manic depression, is a serious brain illness that runs in families and is caused by abnormal brain function. Anyone can get it, but it most often starts in the late teen or early adult years. It is characterized by mood changes that swing from mania (being more active than usual, jumpy, fast-talking, agitated, etc.) to depression (feeling very low, empty; having trouble concentrating; losing interest in fun activities, etc.).

Crazy takes place in the early 1960s when adequate treatment for bipolar disorder was almost non-existent. At that time, patients with bipolar symptoms were either misdiagnosed with schizophrenia, or given the loose diagnosis of "nervous breakdown." This term refers to a sudden, acute attack of mental illness such as depression or anxiety. While it is still commonly used by the general population to describe various degrees of response to chronic stress, it is not acknowledged as a diagnosis in the psychiatric community today.

Psychopharmacology, or the use of drugs to treat mental disorders, has dramatically improved since the sixties. Then, patients were often hospitalized for long periods of time, treated with heavy tranquilizers more suitable for severe psychosis, and given electroconvulsive therapy, or shock therapy. There is now a wide variety of medications available to treat bipolar disorder. Shock therapy is still used today, although usually in conjunction with medications and talk therapy or support groups.

Persons suffering with mental illness in the sixties had few support services and social advocates. In 1979 the National Alliance for the Mentally Ill (NAMI) was founded as an advocacy group for families and people affected by mental illness. On a broader scale, the Americans with Disabilities Act of 1990 also protects the rights of employees suffering from mental disorders. With the help of these legislative actions, the stigma of suffering with mental illness has improved, but has not been entirely eradicated.

Laura was terrified of her mother's condition because it was never explained to her or discussed within the family, and this only served to heighten the stigma that she felt. No one asked her to keep it secret. It was the only way she knew how to survive in an era that did not yet promote open communication, talk therapy, and family counseling. We are fortunate today to have protective legislation, medical advances, and social programs in place that enable many sufferers of mental illness to live normal lives. I hope this book will be instrumental in furthering the dialogue and eliminating the stigma of those suffering from any mental illness, particularly bipolar disorder.

ACKNOWLEDGMENTS

I would like to thank the cluster of dear childhood friends who unwittingly held me together during challenging growing-up years, and whose bonds of friendship endure to this day. Thank you to my husband and sons for making room in our family for my writing passions and whims over the years. A special thanks to dear friend, Carol Baldwin, who suggested that a collection of poems needed to be a novel and who has been my steadfast writing buddy ever since. I also thank dear friends Karol Matthews, Lynn Bonner, Lynn Jerabek, Cindy Biboux, Susan Glassow, and Charles Trevino for reading and commenting on the early stages of the manuscript, providing a cheering squad, and suffering through the submission process with me. I owe a debt of gratitude to Patti Gauch, who went the extra mile with me at a Highlights Foundation workshop and helped me find my YA voice. And I owe a huge thanks to my admirably patient agent, Julia Kenny, whose belief in the manuscript never wavered and who endured an avalanche of Nervous Nellie emails during the submission process. I'd like to thank everyone at Eerdmans who has been so gracious to help me along the way, including Anita Eerdmans, Gayle Brown, Jeanne Elders DeWaard, Katherine Gibson, Ingrid Wolf, Ahna Ziegler, and Jacob Thielman. And finally, a huge thank you and deep gratitude to my fantabulous editor, Kathleen Merz, who pulled words, phrases, and ideas out of me in a way that turned hard work into an enlightening adventure.

LINDA VIGEN PHILLIPS has enjoyed reading and writing poetry throughout her life. Now as a retired teacher she is delighted to have enough time to pursue this passion. *Crazy* is her first novel, drawn from her own experiences growing up in Oregon. She now lives in Charlotte, North Carolina with her husband and within driving distance of her twin sons and grandkids. Visit her website at www.lindavigenphillips.com.